NEVER

DO A

WRONG

THING

MH

ISBN-10: 1726616312
ISBN-13: 978-1726616317

Marcus Herzig
244 Madison Avenue
New York, NY 10016-2817
U S A

www.marcus-herzig.com

For all the boys I've loved before

ONE

When things start going awry is when the story starts, no sooner, no later. That's what Mrs. Bartkowski told us in her Creative Writing workshop, but frankly, that doesn't help me all that much if I can't say for sure when things started going awry. If I were to ask you, Tom, you'd probably say things started going awry the day I was born, and you'd think your blunt force humor was very clever. Maybe if you want to put all the blame on me, you're right. But I like to think it takes two to tangle, and a more nuanced observer might find triggers, trip wires and catalysts all over the place, so I might as well start my version of the story on a Saturday morning in spring that started out like literally hundreds of others before, but not so many after.

Ding-ding-dong, the doorbell went, and even before the final dong sounded, I was already up on my feet and rushing out of my room. "I'll get it!" I announced as I dived down the stairs, as if anyone else would ever react to your signature way of ringing our *ding-dong* bell twice in rapid succession, producing a second *ding* before the *dong*. You were the only person who ever did that. *Ding-ding-dong* was the sound of you and you alone, and it always made me drop whatever I was doing at the time, my homework, my chores, my games controller, to rush to the door like a Pavlovian dog. Minus the drooling.

"Hey," I said, squinting at you as I opened the door. If my dad were writing this story, he'd probably say I was blinded by the bright smile on your freckled face, or by the mesmerizing twinkle in your deep blue eyes or some sappy shit like that. But in reality, it was the early morning sun that was peeking over your shoulder and tickling my face the way the sight of you never failed to tickle my spine.

"Hey yourself," you said. You were wearing your running shoes, red shorts, and a white T-shirt that posed a stark contrast to your sun-tanned skin and dark hair. "You ready?" Without waiting for my reply, you peeked over my shoulder at my dad who was sitting at the kitchen counter, hammering away at his laptop, presumably plotting another bestselling historical murder mystery romance. Behind him, in the back garden, Mom was watering her plants. "Morning, Mr. and Mrs. Fogel!"

As my mom waved at you, my dad said, "Morning, Tom. How's your mom?" What may have seemed like an inconspicuous interest in the general well-being of you mother was actually something much more selfish, and you knew it, too.

"Great," you said. "She's reading your latest book and laughing at all the right places."

Glancing at you over the rim of his glasses, Dad said, "It's a murder mystery. She's not supposed to laugh at all."

"Sorry, Mr. Fogel! Bye!" You tugged on my T-shirt. "Come on, let's go."

"Dad, we're out for a run," I said. "Later!"

"Later," my dad said, sounding heartbroken.

I pulled the door shut and looked at you and the smug grin on your lips. "That was kinda cruel."

"It's called tough love. Your dad's career will never get any-where if he's complacent about his work."

"He's a New York Times bestselling author, but whatever, bro."

"What's the New York Times?" you deadpanned, and for a moment I was genuinely wondering whether you were being silly or serious. Then you cracked up, making me feel stupid for actually thinking you might not know what the New York Times is. "Oh, Timmy," you said wrapping your arm around my neck and ruffling my hair, "you really should see your face sometimes."

"I do," I said. "We have a mirror in the bathroom."

You chuckled and ruffled my hair some more before you pulled me down into a headlock and gave me a noogie. Placing my hands on your sides, I clawed my fingers into your waist, and you immediately started to squeal and squirm because you were ticklish like a little girl. You couldn't have that, of course, because it made you look weak, so you pushed me away. "Are we gonna run or what? Come on!" You dashed off. I followed you down our driveway and caught up with you by the time we reached the sidewalk.

Our regular route was like a trip down memory lane in almost chronological order. A few hundred yards down from my house, we passed our old kindergarten, the place where we first met when we were both four years old. I was a loner, you were the new kid, and you didn't hesitate to sit down and play with me when no one else would. Later on, you made other friends for the both of us, and I never looked back.

We crossed the street and turned the corner into Harbor Boulevard. When we reached the intersection with Madison, we had to sidestep a bunch of flowers and candles resting against a lamp post. A couple of months back, a guy from our school had crashed his car at this intersection and burned to death in the wreckage. He was a senior, so we didn't know him personally, but we'd seen him around campus. The whole school had been talking about it at the time because there was a pretty gruesome traffic cam video of the incident, and even months later, people were still leaving flowers and lighting candles at the intersection, so I guess he must have been pretty popular.

As we left the street and took a turn into the park, we passed by the old chestnut tree near the playground that you had challenged me to climb when we were ten. I didn't want to, but I wanted to disappoint you even less. Before I got to join you at the tree top, I misstepped and fell and broke my leg. To your credit, you visited me at the hospital after school for a week and brought me my homework every day, and I thought that was really sweet. That was when you first said the words to me. "Best friends forever, bro."

We continued on our way past the soccer fields where we had fooled around one day when we were eleven. Tired of playing soccer, we had directed each other to walk across the field blindfolded. It was all fun and games until I inadvertently let you walk headfirst into a goal post, turning you into an instant unicorn. You felt all dizzy and had a headache, so I walked you home where your mom put ice on your forehead. I'm not sure you ever believed me that I didn't let you run into that goal post on purpose. It kinda hurt to know you'd think I could ever do that, that I could ever watch you about to get hurt and do nothing, but after a while I got over it, and we never talked about it again.

Leaving the park at the other end and turning back into the street, we reached our old elementary school and slowed down. We used to get into trouble when we were still students here and climbed the waist-high perimeter wall between the schoolyard and the sidewalk. Our teachers used to freak out because surely we couldn't be trusted to balance on a goddamn wall without falling down, and if we got hurt, the insurance wouldn't pay our medical bills and our parents would probably sue the school. It was the typical stupid, adult, no-fun-allowed type of attitude that we loathed and that didn't make any sense to us, so as soon as we were out of elementary, we made a point of climbing the wall and walking its entire length whenever we passed the school. Sometimes our old teachers would see us and shake their fists at us, but we would just laugh and stick our tongues out at them because we were big boys now and they no longer wielded any power over us. We still climbed that wall every time we came by this place, gleefully like the little boys we once were.

As we reached the end of our round, turning back into Deerfield Street, we had to sidestep a young couple pushing a stroller with a baby boy in it. What was unusual about it, although it shouldn't have been, but to me, even in this day age, it still was, was that they were both men with hipster beards, and one of them had his hand tucked in the back pocket of the other. Once we'd left them behind us, I heard you utter, "Damn fags."

"Why would you say that?" I said in between two breaths.

"Why wouldn't I?" you said, slowing our jog down to a walk.

"I don't know, because it's kinda offensive?"

"It sure is," you said, but you were not talking about your language. "Look, I don't care what kind of perverted stuff people do in the privacy of their own bedrooms, but why do I have to be confronted with it in public? It's bad enough that they get to adopt kids and turn them gay and shit."

Fags. Perverted. Hearing these words from your mouth hurt, and I wondered if you ever would have said them if you'd known about me, but that was a question I wasn't quite ready yet to know the answer to. But this is not where things started going awry. This wasn't new. I had heard you say disparaging things about gay people before, but I'd never called you out on it. I didn't want to wake that sleeping dog, not just because it might bark at me but also because it looked kind of adorable while it was sleeping.

"Oh," I said with raised eyebrows and a challenging smile, "is that how this works now? Gay parents have gay kids?"

You scoffed. "Does the pope shit in the woods? Dogs raise dogs, cats raise cats. Gay parents raise gay kids."

I wasn't even sure if you were really that ignorant or if you were just trolling. "So let me get this straight—no pun intended—if a pair of dogs were to raise a kitten, that kitten would become ... a puppy?"

"Yes," you said, utterly convinced of yourself. "Except two dogs would never raise a kitten because it's not natural. Just like being gay."

"Actually, there are plenty of examples of gay animals. Penguins, turtles, lions and whatnot. Some of them even raise kids together."

You stopped and shook your head. "Fake news, dude."

"No, seriously. Google it."

"And why would I wanna do that?"

"To broaden your horizon and educate yourself," I said. "No wonder you flunked biology."

"Oh, shut up," you said. "Why are we talking about gay turtles anyway? Is there something you wanna tell me?"

"Number one," I said, "you started it, and number two, no, I'm not a turtle."

The word turtle hadn't quite left my tongue when I wanted to kick myself. What was I doing? *I'm not a turtle?* It would have been a great line during open mic at the Chuckle Club, but you weren't chuckling. You looked at me, stone-faced, trying to figure out what the hell I was talking about. Was I trying to be funny? Because you clearly didn't seem to think this was funny, but all it took was an insecure laugh from me and a slap on your shoulder to put you out of your misery and keep you from vocalizing that nagging question in your eyes.

Rolling your eyes and shaking your head, you said, "Speaking of number two, I gotta take the Browns to the Super Bowl, so let's go."

"Urgh! Way too much information," I said with a grimace to conceal my relief that I somehow made us both dodge a bullet that would have gone straight through your head and into my heart.

"Don't be so anal," you said with a dismissive wave of your hand, and I didn't even know what to say anymore.

Eager to change the topic, I said, "So what do you wanna do today?"

"Masturbate under the shower," you said with a feisty grin. When I didn't take the bait, you added, "I don't know. Wanna catch a movie or something?"

"Sure. What do you wanna watch?"

"I don't know, something with tits?"

I rolled my eyes. "Why did I even ask?"

You laughed and punched my shoulder. Grinning, I shrank back. Your chummy shoulder punches had become a bit too boisterous as of late because apparently you didn't know what to do with all that testosterone.

"Let's just go to the theater and see what's playing."

I nodded. "Okay."

"Last to reach your house buys the popcorn," you announced, and before I even got to protest, you were already dashing off, leaving me behind with no chance to catch up.

Two

You pulled the swing door and held it open for me as I walked into the auditorium, holding a tray with two soft drinks, a large bucket of popcorn and a bag of candy for which I had paid a freaking total of $27. To your credit, you had paid $24 for both our tickets. Of course you were going to teasingly remind me of your extraordinary generosity for the rest of the day, and you wouldn't stop until I offered to reimburse you for my ticket, at which point you would scowl at me, pretending to be offended that I would seriously doubt your generosity. It had become kind of a ritual by now because we went to the movies a lot.

You followed me into the dimly lit amphitheater-style 200-seater auditorium that was sparsely crowded with some twenty people, mostly couples or small groups of friends and the odd single, middle aged man. Climbing the stairs toward the mid-section, I was about to enter one of the center rows because it was empty and we liked to sit in the middle of the auditorium, not too close to the screen and not too far away, but from the corner of my eye I saw you keep walking. I stopped and looked at you as you kept climbing the stairs.

When you reached the last row, you turned to look at me, and I followed you because you obviously had no intentions to turn back. By the time I caught up with you, I realized what had made you break our time-tested seating protocol. You proceeded to the center of the row and sat directly behind two girls about our age, a blonde and a redhead.

"Best seats in the house," you announced as you sat down. "Great view."

"Right," I said.

The girls turned their heads and eyed us suspiciously as I took my seat next to you. Then they turned to each other, put their heads together and giggled. Groups of girls always seemed to giggle, and it made me feel kind of envious because you and I used to be like that before the testosterone had kicked in. It also made me feel anxious and self-conscious because I found it painfully easy to assume that if a bunch of girls looked at me and started to giggle, they must have thought I looked funny or I had a massive booger hanging from my nose or something unflattering like that.

"So," you said to me in what barely qualified as an indoor voice, "too bad that Ashley broke up with you, huh?"

I stared at you with my eyes wide open because I had no idea what you were talking about. I didn't know anyone named Ashley and I'd never even been in a relationship.

"You were such a great couple," you said and winked at me, and I was finally beginning to catch on.

"Right," I said, playing along. "I guess it wasn't meant to be."

"Yeah, I guess it wasn't. But hey, at least you've already had a couple of girlfriends. Was she your second or third?"

"Forth," I said proudly, and I immediately regretted it. If I were to present myself as an available bachelor, it begged the question why I couldn't seem to maintain a relationship. If girls kept breaking up with me, then clearly something had to be wrong with me, and if I was the one who had been ending those relationships, then what did that say about my commitment? But then I realized I wasn't the one who was supposed to look good here. Nevertheless, I felt the need to salvage my reputation, so I said, "The one who had to move to Wisconsin, remember?"

"Oh, right, I always forget about her. What was her name again?"

I hadn't been expecting that question, so in order not to thwart the authenticity of my story by taking too long to answer, I blurted out the first name that popped up in my mind. "Winifred."

"Of course," you said slowly, your piercing eyes stabbing me to death. "Winifred."

Being rather more appreciative of my story, our target audience continued to giggle. With a shrug and an awkward smile, I said, "So what about you, Tim?"

"Oh well, you know. It's not easy when you're shy like me. I would really like to have a girlfriend. Someone sweet and gentle and with a great sense of humor. Someone I can spoil and treat like a lady, you know? I just haven't found the right one yet."

"Or she hasn't found you yet," I said. I could tell the girls in front of us were on the verge of cracking up. They were totally on to us, but you didn't seem to care.

"I don't know, maybe I'm just not attractive enough."

Your fake self-pity nearly broke my heart, so I said, "Oh, I think you're very attractive." I wasn't even lying. You looked stunning as always, but then again, I may have been biased.

"You think?" you said with puppy eyes.

"Definitely."

"You're only saying that to make me feel better."

"Is it working?"

You sighed. "No."

I leaned forward and stuck my head between the girls' seats. "Excuse me," I said with the sweetest, most mellow voice I could muster. They both shifted in their seats and turned their heads to look at me, smiling anxious smiles. "My friend here seems to think he's not attractive. Would you mind telling him he's wrong?"

The girls looked at each other and laughed. From the corner of my eye I could tell you were not entirely happy with their response, and I was beginning to feel bad for you. What if they were suffering from a terrible lapse of taste and told you you were ugly? Ready to pick up the pieces of your shattered ego, I saw the blond girl shift in her seat some more to look at you.

"Hello," you said with an awkward grin.

The girl turned back to me and said, "Well, he's not unattractive."

"Oh, come on!" I said, playfully exasperated. "Not unattractive? Is this the best you can do for my friend here?"

With a subtle smile, she looked at you again, then back at me. "Okay, he's kinda cute."

"I'll take it," you said, ripping open the bag of candy. Leaning forward, you held the bag between the girls. "Ladies, be my guest."

"Thank you," the girls said in unison, each taking a piece of candy.

"By the way, my name is Tom," you said, compelling me to add, "And I'm Tim."

The girls giggled again. We got that reaction a lot. Not because Tim was kind of a funny name or anything, but I guess in combination with Tom it was. As the girls chewed on their soft candy with no apparent intention to volunteer their own names, I noticed how you were moving in to ask them, but then the house lights went down and the commercials started to roll. We reclined into our seats and focused on the screen for the next two hours. Or at least I did. The latest addition to the *Maze Runner* franchise was right up my alley, and I'm not gonna deny that it was mostly due to the excellent ensemble cast of highly attractive young male actors. I only wished you could share my sense of bliss, but from the corner of my eye I could see that you spent more time looking at the girls than watching the movie, and several times throughout the movie, you stuck your hand between the girls' seats to offer them more candy. They always accepted your bribes gratefully with silent chuckles, prompting you to cast me contented smiles.

When the movie was over, I got ready to leave but you didn't move. We usually didn't stick around for the credits, but apparently today we did, and it didn't take a rocket surgeon to guess why. It wasn't until the house lights came back on that you rose from your seat, in sync with the two girls in front of us who were doing their very best to pretend they didn't know us after they'd eaten half of *my* candy. Then again, maybe they were just playing hard to get, and I reminded myself that I knew precious little about girls.

"So ladies," you said with a smug grin on your face, "can we invite you to a drink?"

The blonde raised an eyebrow at you. "A drink?"

"Well, a soft drink, of course."

The girls exchanged amused looks. As the redhead shrugged, the blonde turned back to you and said, "Sure, why not?"

"Awesome," you said, nudging me with your elbow.

We made our way outside. Squinting against the gleaming afternoon sunlight, you stopped and turned to the three of us. "So," you said.

The blond girl looked at you. "So what?"

"So, where would you like to go?"

She laughed. "You invite us on a date and you don't even know where you want to go?"

My heart skipped a beat at the word 'date.' While I may have secretly been thinking of my afternoon at the movies with you as a date, I hadn't been expecting it to end up as a double date with you and two girls, but this was clearly what we were heading toward. You couldn't take your eyes off the blond girl, so I was obviously stuck with the redhead, who was quite cute, but from the corner of my eye I could see her eyeballing me from head to toe with a subtle smile, and it made me feel uncomfortably self-conscious. I tried to avoid her gaze, but I failed, and when our eyes finally met there was virtually no reaction. She just kept smiling that subtle, mysterious smile, and the only response I could think of was a grin that I'm sure must have looked just as awkward as it felt.

"My apologies," you said, "but if we'd known we'd be running into you guys today, we'd have reserved a table. Put on nicer clothes, too. Right, Tim?"

"Uh, yeah. Of course," I said, slightly offended by your jab at my timeless shorts and T-shirt combination and trying to remember when I'd last been to a place so fancy they took reservations. Probably two years ago when my parents had taken me out to dinner to celebrate their fifteenth wedding anniversary, a night I'd rather forget. I mean, the food was nice and all, and it was sweet to see how my parents were still in love like a bunch of silly high schoolers. Until they started reveling in their memories, that is. I'm going to spare you the gruesome details, but let me just say I didn't really need to know the exact circumstances of my conception.

"You guys know the Korova?" the redhead asked, and my heart suddenly tried to catch up with all the beats it had previously skipped.

"What's a Korova?" you said, and I was grateful you directed your question at the girls and not at me, relieving me of the dilemma of either having to lie to you that I didn't know or having to admit that I did, which would have inevitably lead to further and more embarrassing questions once you'd seen the place.

"It's a milk bar up on Madison, across from the mall," the blonde says. "They have great milkshakes and pastries."

"Sounds great," you said, but it really didn't, not to me, and my face was on fire as I felt the redhead's piercing glance on my glowing cheeks. I looked at her, and she still had that subtle smile on her round, pale face as if she were able to read my mind.

"Great, let's go," I said, because someone much smarter than me once said offense is the best defense, and so I delved head-first into a potential disaster, only because I couldn't think of an inconspicuous way to avoid it and because I always carried with me the irrational hope that things would never turn out as bad as they could.

I'd never been to the Korova myself, but I had passed the place many times, always casting curious, surreptitious glances inside, catching intriguing glimpses of a colorful, sparkling world crowded with beautiful, self-confident, proud people. It was a world I had recently felt a strange kind of attraction toward, and I'd spent endless hours thinking of, daydreaming of, wanting to be a part of that world, preferably with you by my side. I knew this could never happen, not the way I wished it could, with you being more than just a friend, but I was hopeful you'd enjoy venturing into this world with me, as a tourist, as my guest, one day when I'd be proud to call this world my own. When I had woken up this morning, I wouldn't have dared to dream I'd be able to catch a glimpse of that bright and shiny future before the day was out.

When we reached the place, you were a true gentleman, holding the door open for us with a cosmopolitan smile as if you'd been taking people out for drinks your entire life, but once we made our way inside, your smile congealed into a grimace, and your eyes widened to the size of saucers as you uttered under your breath, "Oh boy."

The Korova's interior was modernistic but simple. Plastic and glass surfaces refracted the bright lights from the rainbow-colored ceiling and made the room distinctly colorful. In contrast, the walls were decorated with larger-than-life black-and-white photographs, very artistic photographs of couples kissing or looking at each other with longing eyes. Nothing wrong with that, but it's worth pointing out they were all gay couples, and you clearly weren't expecting to be taken to a gay bar—a gay milk bar but technically a gay bar nonetheless. The patrons were a colorful mix, both in age and gender. By the window, a lesbian couple was having milkshakes with their two pre-K kids, a boy and a girl. Back in the corner, two guys in their late twenties were looking at us, sipping coffee. In the next booth, two younger dudes were holding hands and looking at a music video on their laptop, sharing one pair of earbuds between them. I immediately fell in love with the place, but I tried not to let it on. At the same time, I tried not to appear as shocked as you clearly were, not only because I wasn't but also because I felt like I owed it to myself to treat sexual diversity the way I wanted everyone to treat it: like it was normal and nothing to crumple one's nose at.

Behind the counter, a bald man in his early forties was operating one of the coffee machines. A white tank top covered his heavily tanned, v-shaped torso, and he wore a pair of black skinny jeans that didn't leave much to the imagination. When he turned around and saw us, his chiseled face lit up and he said, "Why, hello there, kitties!"

"Oh God," I heard you mumble through clenched teeth. I chuckled, and you smiled back at me because you obviously thought I shared your bemusement when in fact I was merely amused by your reaction.

"Hi, Milo," both girls said before they led us to a booth by the window. We sat down, you and I opposite the girls, and before we got to take a proper look at the menu, Milo had left his place behind the counter and sashayed toward us.

"So, my little ones," he said, putting one hand on the back rest behind the redhead, the other on his hip. "What can I do you for?"

I could feel you cringe next to me. Yo were clearly not comfortable in this extremely liberal atmosphere, and I wished this Milo guy would take it a little easy on new and innocent customers like us.

"I'll have a Strawberry Feels Forever milkshake," the blonde said.

"Excellent choice." Milo nodded and looked at the redhead.

"Double Dark Chocolate Shock."

"Oh, that sounds good," I said. "I'll have one, too."

"Of course," Milo said before he turned to you. "And you, sweetheart?"

Glaring at Milo, because you clearly didn't appreciate being called a sweetheart by a gay man, you curtly said, "Diet Coke."

"That's okay, I don't judge," Milo said with a wink. "So, can I interest anyone in some glorious cheesecake? It's homemade by my lovely husband Hans, and I'm totally not exaggerating when I say it's the best cheesecake you'll eat today."

"That's funny," I heard you say, and I braced myself, because from the tone of your voice I could tell you were about to say something you found incredibly clever, but I wasn't sure your audience would agree. Staring at the menu in your hands to avoid Milo's gaze, you said, "Here I was thinking this place only serves fruitcakes."

Blond girl gasped, covering her mouth with her hand. The redhead squinted and looked at *me*, her subtle smile even more subtle than before, and I felt my face flushing like that one time in second grade when I accidentally told the teacher to go screw herself. Between the moment the words had escaped my mouth and the moment I realized she hadn't heard me, I had died a million little deaths, just like I was doing now.

I cast an awkward glance at Milo, and I was surprised to see that he seemed to be the only one who wasn't perturbed by the rudeness of your remark. He put his other hand on his hip now, tilted his head to the side and said, "Aren't you adorable. No cheesecake for you then, I suppose. What about the rest of you?"

"Well," blond girl said, "since Tom here is buying, I'll have some."

"Excellent," Milo said. He turned to redhead and me. "What about you guys?"

"I'll have some as well," she said, and I nodded. "Me too."

"Coming right up," Milo said and made his way back behind the counter.

The blond girl grinned at you. "Thanks, Tom."

"Yeah, thank you, Tom," I said. "That's very generous of you."

Glaring at me, you said, "I'm only buying for the girls."

"Wow, so sexist, but okay."

You turned to the girls. "So ladies, what did you say your names were?"

The girls exchanged amused looks, and the blonde said, "We didn't, actually. But since you're almost asking, I'm Maia."

"I'm Inka," the redhead said.

You looked at me, and I looked back at you. Sensing a laughing fit ready to burst, I tried not to trigger it, so I just shrugged. Looking back at the girls, you said, "You're joking."

Maia frowned. "Um … no? Why, do you think our names are funny?"

"Oh, no, not at all. It's just an unusual combination, that's all. But look who's talking. I mean, we're Tim and Tom, so yeah, never mind." You paused for a moment before you said, "So how are your brothers Aztec and Olmec doing these days?"

The girls looked at each other and both facepalmed very slowly, working very hard not to burst out laughing. I could tell you were just as pleased with yourself as you were with their reaction.

"Don't tell me you've never heard that one before," I said.

With a smile, Maia shook her head. "Honestly, no."

"There you go," I said, nudging you with my elbow. "And to think people say you're not funny."

You looked at the girls and shook your head. "Literally no one has ever said that."

"You are kinda funny," Maia reassured you, making you beam like the sun.

As we waited for our milkshakes, we returned to awkward silence. The girls checked their phones while you looked around the place and stared at the multiple pieces of photographic artwork adorning the walls. One particular black and white poster captured your attention. It showed two females, one black, one white, in an embrace that covered their naked breasts as they engaged in a passionate kiss. You nudged me with your elbow to catch my attention and flicked your head at the poster with a wide, sophomoric grin, which I guess was fair since we were sophomores. With an awkward smile, I shrugged because it was the best innocent response I could think of.

"So, girls," you said. "Are you …" Your voice trailed off and you pointed your finger back and forth between them.

"Are we what?" Inka asked.

"Well, you know."

The girls exchanged confused looks. "We don't, actually," Maia said.

With an awkward grin, you scratched your head. "I'm not sure how to put this."

"Just say the word," I said, trying to put you out of your misery.

"Lesbians," you blurted out, your cheeks turning adorably crimson.

The girls looked at each other for a moment, wide-eyed, before they burst out laughing. No," Maia said. "No, we're not."

You threw yourself back into your seat, visibly relieved. "Oh, thank God!"

"Why?" Inka said. "Would that be a problem?"

"What?" You shook your head emphatically. "Oh, no, not at all. I love lesbians."

Pinching the bridge of my nose, I hoped you weren't going to tell them about the lesbian porn video you had shown me a couple of weeks back.

"I was just thinking, because …" You looked around. "This place is kinda … gay, you know?"

Out of nowhere, Milo shoved a huge tray on our table. "This place is not gay, it's gay friendly, as are most of our customers. Almost all of them." He placed our milkshakes and cheese-cakes in front of us and, finally, he served you your Coke and a bright pink strawberry cupcake covered with rainbow sprinkles. "For you, cupcake. It's on the house."

Looking at the cupcake, you said, "I feel sexually harassed."

Picking up his empty tray, Milo rolled his eyes. "Oh please, don't flatter yourself, sweetie." He turned to us with a wink and a smirk and said, "Enjoy, darlings," before he turned on his heel and sashayed away.

"So, how did you guys like the movie?" I said, trying to steer the conversation away from anything gay, but you didn't play along.

Unwrapping your cupcake, you said, "Honestly, I didn't like it."

"Really?" I said, somewhat disappointed like always when we disagreed on a subject. "Why not?"

You grinned. "Not enough boobs. Too many supposedly sexy young dudes, too few hot young girls."

"To be fair," I said, shaking my head, "it had more female characters than the first *Maze Runner*."

"Even so. It was all so … I don't know. All that oily skin and all those bare arms … I was expecting some of the guys to start making out any moment."

"Disappointed?" Inka asked with a wink.

You snorted. "Hell no. So did you guys like it?"

Thankfully, you directed your question at the girls. It saved me from disagreeing with you and from having to admit I had loved the movie for the same reason you'd hated it.

"I think it was good," Maia said between two bites of cheesecake, and Inka nodded in agreement, sucking on the straw of her milkshake.

"I rest my case," you said. "It was basically a chick flick."

Shaking my head, I chuckled. "By your definition, each and every action movie is basically a chick flick."

You thought about it for a moment, then you looked at me and nodded. "You know what, that's absolutely right. Half naked, sweaty dudes are for girls to flail over. And gay guys, I guess."

Raising an eyebrow, Maia looked at you and says, "Is it just me or am I sensing a lot of homophobic vibes coming from you?"

It was definitely not just her. I was sensing it too, and it kinda broke my heart, but I was grateful she raised the question, because it was something I never could have done. Well, maybe not never, but not now, not yet. Not in public.

Raising your arms in defense, you shook your head. "From me? Not at all. Look, I say live and let live, right? Gay, straight, trans, dog or cat lover, I don't really care what anyone does in their own bedroom or on the kitchen counter or whatever, as long as I'm not forced to watch it or—God forbid—take part in it, you know?"

"So," Maia said, "you're triggered by gay couples kissing in public, is that what you're saying?"

"Honestly, I think even straight couples kissing in public is … I don't know how to say it. Offensive is probably not the right word, but it's not something I need to see. Like, get a room or something, right? I wouldn't start throwing rocks at two people kissing, no matter if they're gay or straight, but don't expect me to cheer them on."

Maia shrugs. "Fair enough, I guess."

All the while I had been staring at you, not sure if I should be impressed or offended by your ability to enshroud your latent homophobia in a camouflage cloak of general antipathy toward public displays of affection and get away with it. It was the pinnacle of your personal perception of what masculinity was or was supposed to be, an outdated ideal, an ancient

NEVER DO A WRONG THING

archetype, a paradigm of centuries past, still prevalent in too many boys and men today. It reminded me of that one time when you spent a weekend in Las Vegas with your parents when you were eight, and upon your return you thought you knew what Paris, Venice, and New York looked like when in fact you knew nothing of the sort. It was adorable in a way, but very childish, just like your views on gay people, although those were only childish and in no way adorable. In fact, it hurt me to hear you express these views with such vigor, and I was dreading the day when I would have to tell you the inconvenient truth about your best friend.

At least you didn't seem to have any qualms devouring your gay cupcake. You even picked the crumbs out of its paper wrapper, so maybe there was still hope. As we ate our delicious cheesecake and drank our milkshakes, you and Maia did most of the talking. Inka and I did most of the listening, chuckling, smirking and subtle smiling. Most of Inka's subtle smiles came flying my way. I kept wondering what she was thinking, and perhaps she was wondering the same about me. What I was thinking, as I watched you interact with Maia and flirt with her to the best of your abilities, was that something was going to change in our lives. I didn't know exactly what or how, but I had a feeling I wasn't going to like it.

THREE

"Hi, Mrs. Fogel," you said with your signature bright smile. "Can I just say you look beautiful today, as always."

Crawling on her knees, her sweatpants stained with dirt and grass, my mom raised her head to glare at you. Brushing a strand of hair from her sweaty forehead with the back of her rubber gloved hand, she said, "Are you mocking me? Because feel free to help me."

With an encouraging smile I offered you the tray full of unpotted red and orange zinnias I'd been holding for my mom, but you ignored me, which had become kind of a habit in the presence of attractive females recently.

"Oh, I wouldn't dare, Mrs. Fogel. Mock you, I mean. I would love to assist your gardening endeavors, though, but unfortunately I have two left thumbs, neither of which happens to be green, I'm afraid. Not that you would need any help, because your flowerbeds look just as stunning as you do. I could only make things worse."

"Who are you, and what have you done with my son's best friend?"

I lowered the tray so Mom could pick up one of the flowers. "Don't mind him, Mom. He's practicing his compliments."

Mom placed the flower in a hole in the ground and covered the roots with soil. "Huh. You might wanna read a book on the topic first."

Casting me a fake frown, you said, "What's a book?"

"She means you should Google it."

"You guys," my mom said, shaking her head. She looked at you with a twinkle in her eyes. "Any particular reason for that sudden interest in your appeal toward the opposite sex?"

We both replied simultaneously.

"No."

"Yes."

Looking back and forth between you and me, Mom said, "Okay, who's lying?"

We both pointed at each other and said in unison, "He is." You scowled at me. "Fake news, yo!"

"You know the proper definition of 'fake news' is factually correct news the person calling it 'fake news' doesn't like, right?"

"That's fake news, too!"

Nodding, I said, "I rest my case."

"You got no case, libtard."

"Careful, Tom," Mom said, an eyebrow raised in warning. Liberal roots ran deep in our family.

"Sorry, Mrs. Fogel," you said. "I would never hold your misguided political persuasions against you. Or let them outshine your splendor."

Casting you a pitying look, she said, "You should really do the Google." She took the tray with the remaining two zinnias out of my hands and placed it on the ground. "Get out of here, you two."

"Ready?" you asked me.

I was already wearing my shorts and running shoes. "Sure."

"Nice day, Mrs. Fogel," you said as we started jogging across our lawn toward the sidewalk.

"I hope I get to meet her one day!" Mom called after you.

"Me too!" you shouted back over your shoulder, sacrificing factual accuracy for a good punchline as you sometimes did and which was actually kind of charming. More charming than your cramped attempts to woo girls, or that one girl in particular, with clumsy compliments, but what did I know? I had never wooed anyone in my life.

We went on our way, jogging down the street. I was smiling because the sun was shining and I was with you, and one of the many things I loved about you was your ability to banter with my parents—and their penchant for entertaining you when you did it. They probably would have viewed you as the perfect son-in-law if I'd been a girl or if you'd been gay, none of which was ever going to be the case. And that was fine. It had to be. No point in ignoring basic facts or trying to change things I knew I couldn't change. If we couldn't be happy together, and I knew we could never be, we could at least be happy, together. That's all I wanted, and I knew I wasn't asking for too much. I wanted you to be happy, I wanted to be happy, and I knew that, ironically, the latter would be harder to control and more difficult to achieve. Why was there always more we could do to make other people happy than we could do to make ourselves happy?

We ran in silence until we reached our old elementary school where we slowed down to climb the wall in retroactive defiance of the yoke of school-authoritarian oppression that we'd long since escaped simply by growing older.

As we walked along the top of the wall in single file, my glance fell upon your brawny, suntanned legs. They had grown a lot stronger since we'd entered high school and you'd joined the school's soccer team. Apart from my crush on you, I'd always had a special crush on your legs because they were long and nicely shaped, not too skinny, not too beefy, and most importantly, not too hairy. Some guys on your soccer team had legs hairier than my dad's, and my dad was basically a chimp.

"Hey, Tim," you said, and I was glad you didn't turn your head to look at me so I didn't have to take my eyes off your legs, "have I told you my parents are going on vacation in a couple of weeks?"

"You haven't, actually. Are they?"

"Well, not exactly a vacation. More like a quick weekend getaway, Friday morning through Sunday night."

"Good for them," I said. "Where to?"

"Palm Springs."

"Nice!"

"Yeah," you said as my eyes slowly made their way up your legs and I silently bemoaned the fact that we didn't live in an age where tighter running shorts were more fashionable. "So anyway, I was thinking, wanna sleep over? We could order pizza and play Xbox all night."

"Sure."

"Or watch porn."

"Awesome," I said with as much enthusiasm as I could muster, which was not a lot, because clearly the porn you had in mind was not the kind that would appeal to me. It briefly occurred to me that if we watched hetero porn, you would probably get aroused and I might catch a glimpse of the inevitable bulge in your pants. I immediately hated myself for having such creepy thoughts, but it was difficult to suppress these thoughts when you started talking about porn while I was staring at your butt. Sometimes it was even difficult not to think about you when I looked at other people's butts, like that one time a few weeks back when I had been sitting in front of my computer in my bedroom, masturbating while watching porn—my kind of porn—and just as I was about to come, your mental image jumped at me from the deepest depths of my subconscious. It was not something I had planned or even would have wished for. In fact, it totally messed up my orgasm because I was trying to push you away, but you wouldn't leave and I lost my focus on the job at hand. It was the sexual equivalent of hitting a wall at a hundred miles an hour, and as if that hadn't been well-deserved punishment enough, I spent the rest of the day beating myself up over what I had done. It's not like I'd never had improper thoughts about you before—or after. Heck, I was staring at your butt right now and wondered what it might look like underneath your shorts. But these were quick, fleeting thoughts, easy enough to push aside, back into the depths of my mind where they belonged. Seeing your face in my mind as I came into my hand felt like I had violated you in a way, even if you didn't know about it and you never would. Immediately afterward, I had taken a shower, feeling like a dirty old pervert for doing what I had done to you. When I met you at school again the next day, I was feeling super awkward, so awkward I could hardly look you in the eyes. But you were your regular self, boisterous as always, joking, laughing, being silly. That's when I realized that thoughts didn't hurt people, only actions did. All I had to do was to make sure my improper thoughts never became actions, and I swore to myself that even if and when I came out to you, as I inevitably would sooner or later, you must never know I ever had feelings for you that went beyond platonic friendship. If you were ever to find out my true feelings for you, I would never be able to look you in the eyes again, and you probably wouldn't even want me to. I was never going to let that happen, no matter how hard it was for me to restrain myself. Best friends forever, bro, no matter what.

"So hey," I said as we jumped back down onto the sidewalk at the end of the wall, ready to resume our jog, "what do you wanna do today?"

You shrugged. "I don't know. What do you wanna do?"

"I don't know. I was thinking maybe catch another movie? Maybe they have something with boobs today."

"That'd be awesome," you said, and I was pleased with myself for catering to your needs even if they didn't exactly align with my own. Then you added, "I'm gonna call Maia. Maybe the girls wanna tag along."

With a frozen smile, I looked past your shoulder through the mesh fence at the school's sports ground to see if someone was practicing archery or throwing the javelin, because it felt like something sharp and pointy had pierced my chest and ripped straight through my heart, but there was no one there. "Uh, yeah," I said. "I mean, yeah. Sure. I mean, why not?" What I was thinking, though, was: *how dare you ruin our one-on-one quality time by asking Maia and Inka to join us?* It made me feel awful for a whole bunch of reasons. First, I hated how I felt compelled to lie to you by feigning enthusiasm for what you clearly thought was a brilliant idea. Second, I hated how you thought it was a brilliant idea. Third, I hated how you managed to make me feel jealous when the last thing I wanted to feel was petty jealousy. I was gay, you were not. Being jealous of some girl didn't even make any sense unless what we were competing for was not your affection but your attention, and let's face it, when we were sitting in a dark movie theater staring at a screen for two hours, there was not a whole lot of conversation going on. But it was the before and after, the buying tickets and popcorn, the instant movie critique right after that was going to be different, and it was also what made going to the movies with you special. Having that taken away, relinquished for the sole benefit of advancing your relationship with Maia, bothered me. Maybe it shouldn't have. It probably shouldn't have, but hey, I was only human and I felt my humanity tested. I couldn't let you think I was jealous, but I was. Having to deal with it on my own with no one to talk to made me feel lonely. It made me feel lonelier than I had ever thought I could in your presence.

"All right then," you said, and I'd be lying if I said I didn't notice that look in your eyes, that bemused, doubtful look as if you could guess there was something I wasn't telling you. Maybe I should have been honest with you, or maybe I needed to work on my lying skills, and I wondered which would be easier. It was a question I couldn't answer on the spot, and I didn't want to give you the chance to press me on this, inadvertently or not, so I punched your shoulder, laughed, and dashed off without a warning. "Last to reach my place buys the popcorn!" I shouted back over my shoulder.

"Son of a bun!" you shouted back, followed by the sound of your feet pounding the asphalt.

Four

"Why, why, why," Milo said, standing by our table, looking at you, one hand on his hips and a twinkle in his eyes. "If it isn't my favorite cupcake. I didn't expect to see you here again so soon. Or ever, really."

We'd switched places this time. Inka and I sat by the windows, you and Maia on the aisle, so I could watch you with one eye and Milo with the other. Reclining and manspreading, one hand on the table, the other on your right thigh, you said, "I'm not scared of you."

"Your manliness is adorable," Milo said. "And I love how you're not letting your bigotry get in the way when it comes to enjoying our gorgeous cakes. Speaking of which, my lovely husband Hans came up with a new recipe for delicious chocolate chip chocolate cake. How's that sound?"

"Totally gay," you said. There was nothing inherently gay about chocolate cake that I could put my finger on, but you were obviously just trying to elicit a reaction. I'm not exactly sure if the reaction you were getting was what you'd been going for. Maia and Inka giggled, and you were pleased with that all right, but Milo put both his hands on his hips, tilted his head to the side, nudged your shoulder with his elbow and said, "Aww, thank you for saying that!"

You shrank back from Milo's touch as if being gay was contagious disease, and I was fine with that because you slid into me, your back touching my shoulder, your thigh touching mine. It gave me a certain level of comfort that you didn't seem to be afraid of physical contact with me in the middle of a decidedly gay establishment, but it was also a sudden, painful reminder of how rare these formerly frequent instances had become. I remembered how often we used to hang out in our respective bedrooms, sitting on the bed, playing video games or having silly conversations, when most often out of nowhere you would pounce on me, wrestle me, test your strength on me, trying to prove to both of us you were the stronger one. Sometimes our roughhousing got painfully rough, but that was fine with me too, because you loved it, and I loved that you loved it. And it's not like I was defenseless like a punching bag. When things got too rough, too painful, I just had to claw my fingers into your ticklish waist and exploit your brief incapacity by straddling you and locking your arms behind your back. The trickiest part was making sure my crotch wouldn't press against your body in case my dick developed a mind of its own and got too excited. But that never happened, and I prided myself on my superhuman self-control. I will admit that I enjoyed holding you like that more than I should have, so much so that I would readily put up with your playful insults. Because of course you owed it to yourself and your male self-image to call me out on my supposedly unfair maneuvers, calling me a girl, a pussy even, and equating tickling with biting or hair pulling. As long as you didn't do it in front of other people, and to your credit you never did, it was a small price to pay for the privilege of pressing my nose against the nape of your neck for a few moments, savoring that enticing mix of your body odor and deodorant. And now that I was thinking about it, your unexpected closeness made me realize how long it had been since we'd had a moment like that. I wasn't sure exactly when it had happened, or how, but at some point things had started to shift away from physical contact. Perhaps it was just part of growing up.

We ordered our chocolate cakes and milkshakes, and when Milo made his way back behind the counter, Inka looked at you and said, "So, what's your issue with gay people?"

Fiddling with your phone, you shrugged and shook your head. "I ain't got no issues."

Inka laughed. "Are you sure?"

"Absolutely," you said. "As long as none of them hit on me, I really don't care what they're up to."

Seeing Inka cast a side glance at me, I pretended I wasn't blushing, and I felt prompted to say, "You mean like religion?" Now you all looked at me somewhat bemused, so I added, "I mean, you're a Christian, right?"

You nod. "So are you, by the way."

"Technically, but not practicing. I haven't been to church in ages. Anyway, my point is, you're a Christian, but you tolerate other religions, right?"

"Sure."

"Like, you don't have a problem with Mormons or something. Or Muslims."

You glared at me a little too long for comfort before you said, "I'm not super fond of Muslims, but as long as they don't make me throw myself into the dirt and pray toward Mecca five times a day, I don't really care. Oh, and bacon. If you want to take away my bacon, I'll fight you to the death."

"To be fair," Maia said, "I'm not aware of any ongoing Muslim campaign to outlaw bacon."

"Or Jews, for that matter," Inka interjected.

Maia nodded. "Right. They just don't eat it themselves. That doesn't mean you can't."

"Come to think of it," Inka said, "when it comes to bacon, you should probably be more worried about radical vegans than Jews or Muslims."

"Right," you said. "Like I said, I don't care what people do in the privacy of their own kitchen, as long as I'm not implicated."

Maia looked at you. "So, do you think you could ever be friends with a Muslim?"

"Or a gay person?" Inka added, and I hated how after asking the question she immediately looked at me with that look on her face where her eyes became little slits and her lips weren't even trying not to smirk as if she thought she knew something she couldn't possibly have known.

Blushing again, I quickly said, "Or a gay vegan Muslim?"

You all laughed, and I joined in, relieved I managed to lighten the mood and wipe that ominous look off Inka's face before you had a chance to notice it.

"Honestly," you said with a pensive look on your face, "I'm not sure. I like to think that I could. You know, like I said, as long as it doesn't affect me. You want to be a vegan, go ahead, knock yourself out, but don't try to make *me* a vegan. I need my bacon and eggs." You paused a few moments, and I was beginning to think you'd never really contemplated the question before. It gave me hope that once you did, you would come to a more agreeable conclusion. But then you said, "You know, one of my favorite quotes goes like this: 'Never do a wrong thing to make a friend or to keep one.' It means stay true to yourself and don't betray your own values just to please someone."

42

"Right," Inka said. "And whose quote is that?"

I had a feeling she already knew the answer.

"Robert E. Lee," you said.

"The Confederate Army guy?" Maia said, raising an eyebrow. "Not sure if that's the best role model."

You shrugged. "Sometimes good people say stupid things, sometimes bad people say smart things. If some nazi says the sky is blue, I'm not gonna disagree with that just because a nazi said it."

"Oh boy," I said, and I did mean it.

Not a moment too soon, Milo returned to interrupt the awkward silence and serve us our milkshakes and chocolate cakes. "There you go, my little kitties. Enjoy."

We dug in, and after a few bites, the verdict that this had to be the best chocolate cake any of us had ever had was unanimous. Well, almost unanimous.

"Pretty good," you said, and considering the circumstances, this could probably be considered the highest praise that could be expected from you. "Almost as good as my mom's."

"His mom's chocolate cake is pretty good," I explained to the girls, much to your satisfaction. "But it doesn't have these huge bits of chocolate. These are not chocolate chips, they're chocolate chunks."

You glared at me, mildly offended. "No one's ever complained about my mom's chocolate cake."

"Oh, I'm not complaining," I said with my best imitation of a contentious smile. "Just stating facts."

You smirked. "No wonder no one likes you."

"I like you," Inka hurried to assure me, and it didn't take Maia a second to agree with her. "I like you, too."

Grinning broadly at you, I shrugged. "See, everyone likes me. Even your mom."

"Yeah, I like you too. Come here," you said, wrapping your arm around my neck and pulling me into a headlock. With your other hand, you gave me a noogie, and it was one of the roughest noogies I could remember. Of course it was. There was no way you were gonna let me win this little chocolate cake skirmish, especially not in front of the girl you were trying so hard to impress. And even though I knew my scalp would be hurting for the rest of the day, I was content to let you win, because it had been such a long time since you'd pulled my head against your flat chest, and for a moment I could even hear your heart beat. To make our little ritual complete, I eventually had to claw my fingers into your side to make you let go of me, but not without jerking your leg and hitting the table, nearly making our milkshakes glasses topple over. Amused by your exaggeratedly pain-stricken face, the girls laughed, and I was happy to call it a draw. With you, a draw almost felt like a victory, but of course it didn't last.

"So, girls," you said, leaning forward as if you had a special secret to share, and deep down in my guts I was beginning to feel queasy. Call it gut instinct, because somehow I knew what was coming. "My parents are going on a weekend break in a couple of weeks and I have the whole house to myself. So I was thinking, how would you like a little slumber party?"

Maia and Inka exchanged a glance, and Maia laughed. "A slumber party? And what, build a fort and play Uno?"

"Or Twister," Inka added with a smirk.

"I was thinking truth or dare," you said, "but whatever you like, girls."

"I'm gonna bring my 8-Ball," Maia said.

Inka put her hand on Maia's shoulder. "I'm gonna bring my Ouija Board."

I'm not sure what was riding me, but I felt everyone was just blurting out their most preposterous ideas at this point, so before I even knew what I was doing, I said, "We can paint our toe nails!" It was probably the gayest thing I had ever uttered in your presence, emboldened by the lighthearted and, I assumed, humorous mood. The initial reaction I got was not surprising. All three of you stared at me, incredulous, bemused, not sure if I was being serious or silly. To put you all out of your misery, I put on the silliest grin I could muster, and after a few excruciatingly tense moments, the girls burst out laughing. You took a second longer to accept my joke, reckless as it might have been, for what it was. With a grin that was half benign and half revengeful, you raised your arm, trying to pull me into another headlock, but my scalp was still burning from the previous noogie, so I leaned away from you and raised my own arm in defense. Naturally, you couldn't let me get away with making fun of your masculinity, or even my own, so you punched my arm. Hard. Trying not to wince, I made a mental note to put on a shirt before I stepped out of the bathroom after taking a shower in the morning so no one would ask me inconvenient questions about the bruise on my arm.

"So you're coming too?" Inka said in my direction. The answer should have been obvious by now, but she seemed eager to obtain firsthand confirmation.

"In fact, up until a minute ago I thought I was the only one coming," I said with a nod, trying not to sound bitter, because our playful banter notwithstanding, hearing you invite the girls to your sleepover that I thought was going to be *our* sleepover felt like an ambush in the dead of night with someone jamming a knife into my stomach and slowly turning it counterclockwise. I would have appreciated if you hadn't ambushed me like that, if you'd waited for a better moment, maybe when we were alone, relaxing, sitting on your bed or mine and watching TV or playing video games, and you'd gently nudged me with your elbow and you'd taken the time to show me your nice, sharp, shiny knife and told me you were going to stab me with it very gently and then slowly turn it counterclockwise. It would have hurt just the same, but at least I would have had time to brace for the impact. Nevertheless, I was a good sport, or at least I tried to be. I liked the girls, and I didn't really mind spending time with them—and you. I especially liked how you were not afraid to make a complete fool of yourself in your awkward attempts to impress Maia or to make her laugh. It reminded me of a version of you I hadn't seen in a long time. Back when we were eleven, twelve, thirteen, you didn't give a damn what people were thinking about you. You were just being your silly self, always up for mischief, always trying to make *me* laugh, and man, you were so good at it. But that was then, and this was now. We were no longer twelve, and you had taken to trying to impress other people. I liked to think it was because you knew you no longer needed to impress me and not because you no longer cared about what I thought about you. I know you did, although I wondered if you still would if you knew what I really thought about you in the privacy of my bathroom.

When I focused back on the here and now where playful banter prevailed, I caught Inka staring at me across the table, again with that subtle smile on her lips, and I responded with an awkward grin fueled by the uneasy feeling that she was probably a witch who could read every single one of my thoughts.

FIVE

"Can I ask you something?" I said, leaning against the door frame to the laundry room in our basement. I wasn't sure what to do with my hands, so I put one on the door frame above my head, the other I put in the front pocket of my jeans. Then I pulled it out again and put it in the back pocket instead.

Mom cast me a brief glance and picked a yellow T-shirt from the huge pile of dirty laundry on the floor, held it against the neon light to check how dirty it was and tossed it into one of three baskets. "Sure," she said casually, and I secretly admired how she managed to pretend it was no big deal that I came to seek her out in the privacy of our laundry room to ask her something when I could have just asked her the same thing much less theatrically at any other time or place.

"So …" I cleared my throat, struggling to find the right words. "You and dad, how long have you been married again?"

Mom raised an eyebrow, confused and possibly mildly offended I would ask her that when the fact that I had been conceived in their wedding night was brought up like clock-work at every single one of my birthdays. "Seventeen years," she said, "as you should know."

"Right," I said. There was no way I could bullshit my mom, so I just blurted out, "You ever get jealous?"

Mom put the blouse she'd just picked up down again and laughed. "Let me tell you something about your father, honey. He's never looked at another woman after he first asked me out, and not even before, as far as I can tell. Why would you even ask me something like that?" A frown clouded her face and she looked me in the eyes. "Wait, is there something you know that I don't?"

"What?" I said, shaking my head. "No! I mean … maybe jealous isn't the right word, but I can't think of a better one. Resentful maybe. Or suspicious. I don't know. Anyway, I'm not talking about a secret love affair with another woman or anything."

"Well, that's a relief," Mom said, not sounding very relieved at all.

"I guess what I'm asking is, do you ever feel jealous or suspicious or resentful of something but you know exactly you really have no reason to feel that way? Because it's, like, totally irrational or something? You know what I mean?"

Mom continued sorting the laundry, pensive and very slowly. She shook her head. "I don't, actually."

Frustrated with my own inability to express myself properly, I let out a sigh. As I thought about a way to ask a better question, Mom picked up a frilly blouse, and it was just the clue I needed. "Do you ever feel jealous of Georgiana Tinderbottom?" I asked, referring to the heroine of my dad's Victorian murder mystery romance series that had paid for Mom's washing machine, my Xbox, and pretty much everything else we owned.

Mom laughed out loud. "Georgiana Tinderbottom isn't real, honey!"

"For someone who isn't real, Dad seems to spend an awful lot of time with her."

"Huh," Mom said, throwing her blouse in one of the laundry baskets. "That's true, I guess. But no, I'm not jealous of her."

"Why not?"

She smiled. "Because he doesn't buy her drinks at a bar, he doesn't take her out to fancy dinners while I sit at home eating mac and cheese, and he doesn't spend the night with her in sleazy motel rooms."

"Except when he attends one of his writers conferences. And how often does he stay up until two or three a.m. writing while you're asleep in your bedroom? That's time he's spending with Georgiana that he's not spending with you, isn't it?"

"Honey, I'm not sure what you think is going on in the bedroom of a married couple of seventeen years on a Wednesday night, but if it's three a.m., I'm asleep and I don't really care if your dad is asleep next to me or sitting in his study picking out fancy dresses for Georgiana Tinderbottom. It's about quality, not quantity. Quality time, I mean. We're very lucky your dad can make a living, and a very decent living at that, without having to leave the house for ten hours a day. Most wives don't get to spend nearly as much time with their husbands as I do, and I'm very grateful for that, but I don't have to sit on his lap twenty-four hours a day. God forbid, nobody wants that. Your dad doesn't, and I don't. We all need our own time, where we can be our own person and do our own stuff, be it planting flowers or writing books. That's not only healthy, it's crucial to keep a marriage alive. So, as long as the ladies your dad spends his time with only exist in his head, I have no problem with that at all. You know what I mean?"

"I guess," I said with a shrug.

"But this isn't about me and your dad, is it?"

I shook my head.

"So whom are *you* not jealous of?"

I felt heat rising to my face, and I knew I needed to tread carefully. Like everyone else, Mom didn't know I was gay, at least not officially. I think she may have had an inkling by now. She had never asked me about girls. I swallowed, cleared my throat and said, "Like I said, jealous probably isn't the right word. It's … it's these two girls we met at the movies the other week, remember?"

"I remember," Mom said with a smirk as if she knew exactly where this was going. It probably wasn't too hard to guess.

"Right, so anyway, they're really nice and everything, but now Tom keeps inviting them along to everything we do. I mean, everything we used to do alone, you know?"

"And it bothers you."

I sighed, leaning my head against the door frame and closing my eyes. "I don't know."

"Come on," Mom said, continuing to sort the laundry, "let's be honest now. It bothers you. Otherwise we wouldn't be having this conversation, would we?"

I sighed again. "Okay, it bothers me, all right? But I know it shouldn't."

"Why not?"

"Because it was just a matter of time for him to find a girl-friend, so I knew it was coming. And besides, it's not like I called dibs on him and have a right to claim all of his attention or anything."

Mom nodded with a sympathetic smile. "So is he spending time with her instead of you now or is he still spending the same amount of time with you, but now there's someone else around?"

I shrugged. "Yes. No. I mean, the latter. But it's not gonna stay like that, is it? I mean, he and Maia aren't even an item yet, but once they are, that's gonna change, I suspect. They're gonna want to spend more time alone together, just the two of them. And I wonder how I'm gonna deal with it when that happens."

"Honey," Mom said, picking up another T-shirt, "you're gonna deal with it just fine."

"You think?"

She nodded. "I'm sure. I'm not gonna tell you it's going to be easy, because it probably won't be, but you're gonna be fine. Look, your dad and I have been married for seventeen years, but we both still have some of the same friends we had before we got married. Sure, we don't spend as much time with them as we did in high school, but again, it's about quality, not quantity. You and Tom have been best friends almost your entire lives, and I'm sure nothing is ever going to change that."

I wished I could share her confidence about our friendship, but I just said, "Okay. Thanks, Mom."

She looked at me, her smile reluctant, almost suspicious. "Is there anything else you want to tell me?"

I shook my head, and I wasn't even lying. There were things I probably should have told her, but I didn't want to. Not now. Not yet.

"No, I'm good," I said, trying to sound cheerful.

"You know you can tell me anything that's on your mind, right?"

I knew I probably could, and I wasn't worried my parents might disown me once they found out I was gay. I was going to tell them eventually, when the time was right. "I know, Mom. Thanks again."

I made my way upstairs, and just as I was about to close my bedroom door behind me, my phone rang in my pocket. A look at the screen told me it was you.

"Hey," I said.

"Hey."

I dropped down on my bed and looked at the ceiling. "What's up?"

"Nothing. I just wanted to check on you. See if you're okay."

"Sure I'm okay," I said, and I honestly had no idea what you were talking about. "Why wouldn't I be?"

"I don't know. You seemed kinda quiet today."

My heart was pounding in my chest, torn by conflicting feelings of love and loathing. The loathing was all self-loathing. I hated how I was unable to conceal my feelings when I needed it the most, how people could read me like an open book and take a glimpse deep into my soul, making me feel exposed and vulnerable. The love I felt was all for you and your unexpected ability to pick up on my state of mind. It almost made me feel special. Special, and also pretty awkward because I had no easy answer for your question.

"You think?" I said.

"You barely said a word the whole time at the Korova, so I was wondering if everything's okay."

"Yeah, sure. It's just, you know, the bigger the group, the quieter I get. You may have noticed that before."

"Right," you said, sounding not entirely convinced. "I was just wondering if maybe you don't like the girls or something."

"What? No! Why would you even say that?"

"I don't know. Like I said, you seem awfully quiet when the girls are around."

"To be fair," I said, "you and Maia usually drive most of the conversation."

You chuckled. "Are you jealous?"

I scoffed.

"You're jealous," you crowed.

"No, I'm not," I said, and I hated you so much for forcing me to lie to you. "Don't be stupid."

You were laughing your ass off by now, which was as annoying as it was charming because I loved making you laugh. "Hey, wanna know something?"

"I wanna know everything. What is it?"

"But don't get jealous, okay?"

"I'm not jealous!" I shot back at you, and I wished this would have been a face-to-face conversation so I could slap your head.

"All right, all right," you said. "When I walked Maia home after the Korova ... we kissed."

"Oh no, you didn't," I said with a forced laugh because under no circumstances could I allow myself to let you know about the searing pain I was feeling in my heart.

"I totally did, though."

"And?"

"And what?"

"And how was it?" I said, secretly hoping that Maia'd had onion soup with six cloves of garlic for dinner last night, and that she had burped right into your mouth.

"It was very sweet, but I think it's because she was chewing gum. Strawberry. And guess what, after our first kiss, the gum ended up in my mouth."

I scowled. "That is so disgusting!"

"Not at all. It was, like, totally hilarious. And awesome, because I had to kiss her again to return it to her. And then we both almost died laughing."

"Wow," I said because I can't come up with a more eloquent response, but to my defense, I totally meant it.

"I know, right?"

"So I guess you're officially an item now, huh?"

"I guess," you said, chuckling. "I'm gonna meet her parents on Tuesday."

"Wow," I said again. Things seemed to be moving at a nauseating pace now. "Do I need to buy a tux?"

There was a moment of silence before you said, "What?"

"A tux. For the wedding?"

You laughed. "Don't be an idiot. She's helping me with my English essay that's due next week, that's all."

"Oh, okay. That's great," I said because I got an A in English and when I had offered to help you with your essay the other week, you'd said you were good.

There was another moment of awkward silence as my brain was working overtime to come up with something I could say to change the topic, but you beat me to it. "So what do you make of Inka?"

"Inka? I don't know. She's … nice, I guess?"

"She's more of the quiet type. Like you, you know? I guess that's why she's so into you."

"Into me?" I said. "What the hell are you talking about?"

"Dude! How can anyone be so clueless? Haven't you noticed how she keeps looking at you?"

Oh, I had noticed. She kept looking at me as if she were reading my mind like an open book and also as if she were a more attentive reader than you were, with an uncanny ability to read between lines she wasn't even supposed to see. "How's she looking at me?"

"Are you blind? She looks at you the way you look at pizza. She wants to eat you up and lick her fingers."

I cringe. "That's creepy."

"No, it's not, it's awesome! She's totally into you. You should ask her out."

"Ask her out? I don't even know her!"

"What are you talking about? Of course you know her. We've been to the movies twice and had milkshakes and cakes afterward. Plus, she's the best friend of my girlfriend."

I felt another sting to my bleeding heart when you casually said the g-word as if you'd been dating Maia for two years when in reality, you probably didn't even know her birthday or her favorite color or food or what the name of her favorite cuddly toy was when she was a kid. You know, all the things I knew about you.

"I don't know."

"Trust me," you said, and I could virtually hear the smug grin on your face. "I know what's good for you."

I pinched the bridge of my nose and exhaled slowly, trying not to burst into tears. I don't know how I made it through the rest of the call, and when we finally hung up, I dropped my phone next to me on the bed and stared at the ceiling. There was a lump in my throat that I tried to swallow, but it didn't budge. A feeling similar to brain freeze when you've eaten too much ice cream too fast was throbbing behind my eyes. I rubbed my temples to make it go away until I realized the pain came from whatever muscles were involved in holding back my tears. Taking ever deeper breaths through my nose ever faster, I was fighting a losing battle, and when I finally gave in to the undeniable truth that the entirety of my existence was suffering, I rolled over on my side, pressed my face into my pillow and surrendered. Unbearable pain ate its way through my veins and consumed my body like acid, burning, searing like hellfire, condensing into a deluge of saliva, snot, and tears. Once the tears were flowing, there was no holding back. Rocked by spastic sobs, I wrapped my arms around my pillow pretending it was you, squeezing it, holding on to it because I needed to hold on to something and I couldn't hold on to you.

Six

"Okay, super juicy, super tasty burgers coming up in a minute," you said, wielding your tongs like a true BBQ champion, proclaiming your manliness like thousands of generations of men before you by ritually roasting meat over open flames. From your patio, we were overlooking your back garden, the garden of our childhood where we used to play Frisbee, where that old swing set still stood that we used to spend so many hours on until we grew older and upper and too cool and we removed the swings to use the frame as a soccer goal. Summer had made an early entrance, with temperatures pushing ninety degrees on this Saturday in early May, and you were dressed accordingly— just shorts, flip-flops, and an apron that had *Eat My Meat* printed on it. The apron was your dad's, obviously, who was notoriously well known for his crude humor, but you were more than happy to wear in front of the girls. I wasn't sure their reaction—hysterical laughter—was exactly what you'd been aiming for, but you were a good sport about it, winking at them and flexing your bare arm muscles which resulted in more laughter that I joined in more loudly than honestly to conceal my true thoughts about you and your meat. As you kept flipping our burgers, you were being closely watched by three pairs of hungry eyes. While the girls enjoyed your exaggerated antics that belied your manliness as you shrieked like a girl whenever a rogue spark escaped the coal fire and hit your naked skin, I took silent delight in casting furtive glances at you with my sunglassed eyes, eating up your mouthwatering, naked, V-shaped torso.

"Oh shoot!" you suddenly said and you ran inside, tongs still in hand. The girls and I exchanged bemused looks, and our best guess was that you had to use the bathroom real bad, but a minute later you were back with an open bottle of beer. "Almost forgot the most important ingredient."

I looked at you. "Where'd you get the beer?"

Rolling your eyes, you said, "The fridge, duh! Anyone want some, just help yourselves."

"Won't your dad, like, get mad if we drink his booze?"

"Don't be such a square," you said. "There are five crates in the basement. No one's gonna notice if a couple of bottles go missing."

"I'll have one," Inka said, rising from her chair. She looked at Maia. "You?"

"Sure."

"Tim?"

"Uh, yeah, sure."

As Inka made her way into the kitchen, you hovered over the grill, ready to douse our burgers in beer. You put your thumb over the opening of the bottle, but you tilted it too quickly. Beer foam sprayed all over our burgers and into the flames, covering you in a dense cloud of steam and swirling charcoal ash, and I felt bad for secretly hoping your neighbors would call the fire department on us.

"Fuck," you said, coughing and putting the bottle on the small table next to the grill. Waving your free hand to disperse the cloud, you flipped our burgers once, twice, three times before you took them off the grill, followed by the roasted buns.

We ate and drank, and despite the specs of charcoal dust, the burgers were surprisingly good. The first few swigs of my beer tickled the back of my throat, but I quickly got used to the bitter taste and finished my bottle first. The mood of relaxed and lively banter continued throughout our meal with you and Maia doing most of the talking. We eventually retreated to the living room, and much to my chagrin, you changed into a pair of jeans and a T-shirt. Over more banter and more beer, we decided to watch a movie on Netflix. With you and the girls occupying the sofa, I snuggled up on the armchair that was placed at an angle so I could easily look at the TV and cast the occasional furtive glance at you. The movie was a terribly cheesy teenage rom-com, and I didn't even bother to follow the plot, because the romance that was flourishing on the sofa was enough for me to deal with. At first, Maia leaned her head against your neck, then you wrapped your arm around her shoulders. By the time the end credits started to roll, your eyes were closed and your mouths wide open, engaged in heavy kissing.

"Get a room!" I said, and I thought I was making a clever joke until you let go of her, looked at her with a dreamy smile and said, "Good idea, what do you think?"

Maia responded with a chuckle, and you took that as a yes, so you grabbed her hand and pulled her out of the room.

"Wow," I said to no one in particular. "Didn't see that one coming."

Inka scoffed. "Really? You didn't? You've been watching them closer than the movie."

Feeling caught, I decided to flee forward and deadpan, "Movie? What movie?"

She chuckled, and before we had time to embrace the awkward silence, you stuck your head back in and said, "Tim? You got a minute?"

It seemed like I had a lot of minutes, way more than I ever would have asked for, but I just said, "Sure," and followed you into the kitchen where you awaited me with a wide grin and a big bulge in your pants.

"Dude," I whispered, "what the hell are you doing? Don't leave us alone down here!"

You scowled at me. "What the hell are you talking about? Where did you think this evening was gonna go?"

Stunned and at a loss for words, I wondered what I *had* been thinking where this evening was gonna go.

"Don't waste that chance now," you said. "She's totally into you. You guys can take the guest bedroom. Fresh sheets and everything." You put your hand in your pocket and pulled out a condom. Before I could protest, you slipped it into my pocket, put your hand on my shoulder, leaned into me and whispered, "Now let's go pop those cherries."

I cringed, and I'm not sure if it was your crude language or the absurdity of the situation that I found more disagreeable. It didn't matter much either, because after a little squeeze of my shoulder, you were gone and I was alone, facing a situation I hadn't been expecting to find myself in in a million years. I opened the fridge and grabbed another beer. I'd already had more than enough, but I needed something to hold on to.

When I returned to the living room, Inka had relocated to the vacated sofa, and she welcomed me back with a smile on her lips and the TV remote in her hand. "You got your marching orders?"

"What?" I said, my ears burning up because clearly Inka had a better grasp of the situation than I did.

"Never mind," she said and patted the empty space next to her. "Come sit."

I did as I was told, because that was obviously what everyone expected me to do today. Or any day, for that matter. I plopped down next to her, but I kept a safe ten-inch distance, enough not to seem as randy as you, but not so far away as to make it look like I thought she had cooties. Inka pressed a button on the remote and we watched an episode of *Big Mouth*, a cartoon series about a group of hormone-driven, pubescent 7th-graders, and it was full of off-color humor about teenagers and their challenging, intricate relationships with their penises, vaginas, and body fluids. It was as funny as it was awkward. We both laughed and giggled and chuckled, but it was hard to ignore that the topic of sex hung in the air like a thick blanket on a sultry summer night, suffocating, constricting, making my heart beat not with excitement but with anxiety. Things got worse when Inka released a contented sigh and leaned her head against my shoulder, and I had nowhere to run. I tried not to flinch, not to shy away from her touch, because I didn't want to offend her. I liked her. I liked her quiet but attentive personality, and I liked that she seemed to like me, but the thought that she might be expecting something of me that I couldn't provide freaked me out like a dog when the car pulls into the vet's parking lot. I put my arm on the backrest of the sofa because I didn't know where else to put it, and when Inka snuggled up even closer, my hand slipped down onto her shoulder against my will. Maybe it was because I wanted her to like me, even if it was in a way I could never reciprocate, maybe it was because I didn't want her to dislike me. I wondered if you ever felt that way when we were sitting next to each other on my bed playing Xbox and I *accidentally* sat so close to you that our legs touched and I pretended I neither noticed nor cared, hoping that neither would you. I never did it because I secretly hoped that an innocent touch would lead to something lewd, I did it because I enjoyed our closeness and I knew it was the closest you and I would ever get. Maybe Inka's head against my shoulder was just as innocent a sign of affection and nothing more.

I obviously knew nothing about girls. It didn't take long for Inka to move in and snuggle up ever closer. At first, her hair brushed against my neck, then she put her hand on my chest and lifted her head, looking at me with wistful eyes. Her parted lips were seeking mine, and I didn't know what else to do but smile awkwardly. As a reaction it was all too natural but also all too easy to misinterpret as approval, as an invitation even, so Inka's hand wandered up behind my neck and gently pulled my head closer until our lips finally touched. From upstairs I heard you and Maia laugh, and I was convinced you were laughing at me. I didn't want you to laugh at me, I didn't want anyone to laugh at me, so I surrendered myself to this overwhelmingly absurd situation. I parted my lips and invited Inka's tongue in, warm and wet like a feverish snake, non-venomous but nonetheless terrifying to an ingenuous first-time visitor to the jungle of love. The moment our tongues touched, a dam broke, and I was flooded with Inka's unleashed desire. Without interrupting our tongues' awkward mating dance, she rose, straddled me and sat down on my lap. Kissing me and running her hands through my hair, she grinded her crotch against mine. One hand on her neck, the other one rubbing her back, my heart was racing in my chest, and I was taking deep breaths through my nose. When after a long minute or two our lips finally parted, Inka kissed my cheeks, my neck, and my ear as I pressed my face against her shoulder and my hand slowly, cautiously touched one of her breasts. I squeezed the soft tissue, unsure if I was too brisk or too timid, and Inka softly moaned into my ear, her warm and humid breath sending a shiver down my spine.

"Oh God," she whispered, her hand grabbing a tuft of my hair and pulling it gently.

Feeling pressured to respond, I stammered, "I ... don't know."

She chuckled and grabbed my face with both hands, kissing me on the forehead, the nose, the lips again, still grinding her crotch against mine. Her lips made their way across my face again, and when they reached my ear, Inka whispered, "Should we move to a more comfortable location?"

I was as terrified as I was intrigued. Even if my dick remained unresponsive for now, the unprecedented intimacy with another person was having an effect on me. Inka was clearly willing to go a long way with me, maybe all the way, and I found myself in a situation that I hadn't only never expected to find myself in but that might never ever happen again, so I nodded. Inka dismounted me and took my hand. We got up, grabbed our backpacks off the floor and made our way upstairs. When we reached the landing, I heard a noise coming from the bathroom down the hall. The door to the guest bedroom was ajar. "This is us," I said and motioned her forward. Before I followed her into the room, I heard a door open. I turned my head to see you emerge from the bathroom, wearing nothing but a pair of tighty-whities, shaped into a tent by your massive erection, and I finally felt blood flowing into my own dick. When you saw me, you gave me a thumbs-up and a smug, boisterous grin as you disappeared into your bedroom and closed the door behind you. For the first time today, I felt a hint of sexual arousal, so I'd better put it to some use while I could. I entered the guest bedroom where Inka was sitting on the bed with a misty eyed smile. I closed the door and sat next to her, and before we allowed awkward silence to destroy the dynamics of the situation, we turned toward each other, wrapped our arms around each other, closed our eyes and kissed. It was a mutual maneuver, not initiated by one person and simply reacted to by the other. At this point, it felt like something we both wanted.

We touched. We kissed, taking deep breaths through our noses. I slid my hands underneath her T-shirt and cupped her breasts. She pulled my T-shirt out of my pants and over my head. I did the same with hers. As soon as our lips touched again, my hands found the fastener of her bra on her back. It took me a lot of nervous fiddling, and when I finally managed to unfasten it, my hands made their way to the front, and I carefully slid my thumbs between her loosened bra and her breasts. Her nipples were cold and firm like rubber.

I wondered what your nipples might feel like.

I was thinking of you the whole time, wondering if your lips felt as fleshy and warm as Inka's, and if your tongue was as delicate and nimble. I wondered where your tongue was at right now, where your hands were at, whether or not you were already completely naked. Not only did I wonder. I imagined.

Thinking of you naked and aroused helped my own state of physical excitement, but the fact that I kept thinking of you while making out with Inka made me feel like a liar, a cheater, a terrible human being, and my mental confusion encroached my physical arousal. I was torn between hard and soft, hot and cold, horny and horrible. When we had finally shed all our clothes, I rolled over and reached for my pants to get the condom you'd given me. You. I forced myself to keep thinking of you, and I shuddered when Inka spooned me, pressing her breast against my back and rubbing my dick with her hand.

I was almost hard. Hastily, clumsily, I tore the wrapper open and pulled the condom out. Back on my back, I put the condom on while Inka kept kissing me, but it took forever because my hands were shaking and my dick felt like Jell-O. When I was finally done, I pushed Inka over on her back. She spread her legs and guided me, gently, but the moment my dick touched her vagina, it retracted like a snail's tentacle and shriveled away. Cold sweat on my flushing face, I tried to get it up again with my hands, with my thoughts, my dirty thoughts of you, but nothing helped. Embarrassed, humiliated, I tried to avoid Inka's sympathetic but pitiful gaze as she grabbed my hands and pulled me down. She kissed me, rubbing my back and kneading my butt as she grinded her crotch against mine. She was trying to reignite that spark of physical arousal in me again, but to no avail, and when the condom finally came off and lingered between us, discarded like a candy wrapper on a schoolyard, all tension left my body and I collapsed onto her, pressing my face into the pillow next to hers, my body rocked by miserable, pathetic sobs that none of her gentles kisses and finger strokes across my back could soothe.

"Shhhh, it's okay," she cooed into my ear, and maybe she was right. Maybe it was okay. It had never been meant to be in the first place, but the truth hit home harder than I ever could have imagined. It was a punch to the gut, a slap to the face of everything I wanted and everything I wanted to be, and a wake-up call to the undeniable reality of what I had always known: I was in love with you.

SEVEN

I always hated waking up, even on a normal day. To me, sleep had always been the ultimate state of peace, freedom and happiness, because no matter what kind of crap was going on in my life in the real world, when I was asleep, it all fell away from me. I didn't have to make any decisions, and nothing I did in my dreams mattered. Maybe I was lucky that I'd never been one to bring my day's problems into the night, into my dreams. Even in my darkest hours, I never let reality pervade my dreams. It's not that I never had any nightmares, but my nightmares were never triggered by real life events, at least none that mattered. For better or for worse, neither were my dreams. My sleep was my castle, and in my dreams, I was king. Waking up was like having my government overthrown, my power usurped by outside forces I thought I'd been living in peace and harmony with. What was devastating was not the dissolution of peace and harmony but the sudden awareness that my freedom had always been a delusion.

This was not a normal day.

Inka and I woke up back to back, with two feet of space between us like a married couple of seventeen years, although maybe that's unfair toward my parents. They'd been married for seventeen years, and if my mom was to be believed, their marriage was reasonably happy. Then again, their sex life was probably more successful than mine.

I lay awake for a long time, horrified that the worst night of my life hadn't been a terrible nightmare but a terrible reality. I wanted to get up, get dressed and run away before anyone saw me, but I was too afraid to wake Inka and having to look her in the eyes. Maybe I should have just lain here, pretending to be asleep, waiting for Inka to get up and sneak out of the house when she was taking a shower. I wondered if she was already awake, waiting for me to get up and take a shower so she could sneak out of the house. I had to take a look.

The moment I slowly raised my head to peek over my shoulder, she turned her head and looked me right in the eyes.

"Hey," she said softly, as if she were afraid I'd burst into tears if she spoke too loudly. I might as well have.

"Hey," I said, rolling over on my back, rubbing my eyes and groaning.

"You okay?"

I shook my head. "I have a headache the size of Catalina."

"Too many beers?"

More like too many beers plus a traumatizing experience, but I just nodded.

"Poor you," she said, reaching over and ruffling my hair. I wasn't sure if I should find it patronizing or endearing, but I gave her the benefit of the doubt.

We got up and got dressed. As Inka made her way downstairs to the kitchen, I headed for the bathroom across the hall, toothbrush in hand. Just as I was about to enter, you emerged from your bedroom, pushed me into the bathroom, followed me inside and closed the door. You were wearing shorts and a T-shirt, and your bedhead looked like it had been quite a night.

"Dude," you said with a wide grin, "how awesome was that?"

I shrugged. "I don't know, how awesome was it?"

"It was super awesome. *She* was super awesome. I don't know, either she's a natural talent or she must have done that kind of thing before."

"That kind of thing?"

"Yeah. You know, sex."

"Right," I said, squeezing toothpaste onto my toothbrush. As I leaned over the sink, starting to brush my teeth, you stood next to me, pulled out your dick and started peeing into the toilet bowl next to the sink. I didn't even have to turn my head. I could see your dick and balls in the mirror, and I tried not to think about how this was probably the closest I'd ever get to your junk.

"So how did it go with Inka?"

Grateful to have a toothbrush in my foamy mouth, I shrugged and grunted something that could have meant anything from 'awful' to 'all right' to 'awesome.' As expected, you chose to hear 'awesome.'

"Did you pop that cherry?"

I glared at you in the mirror, rolled my eyes and shook my head.

You lost your grin. "Is that a no?"

I took the toothbrush out of my mouth, spat foam into the sink and said, "That's a 'don't talk like that.'"

"Talk like what?" you said, frowning.

"Like cheap porn or something."

You laughed. "What do you know about porn?"

"More than you, probably." That might even have been true, although I was pretty sure we were talking about very different kinds of porn.

Laughing again, you shook off the last drops and put your junk away. "Look at you," you said, putting your unwashed hand on my shoulder. "Still waters run deep, huh?"

"You have no idea." I turned my head to look at your hand on my shoulder. "But could you not wipe your piss fingers on my shirt?"

"Oops, sorry," you said, and you being you, you started ruffling my head with both your hands.

Dropping my toothbrush in the sink, I ducked away. "Dude, you're so disgusting!"

Howling with laughter, you tried to slap my arms and face but I swatted your hands away. "Stop it, man!"

"All right, all right, sex machine. Come on, let's have breakfast with our girls."

"Let me take a shower first. I'll be right down."

"Hurry up," you said and slapped my butt. I wished I could have found your plump kind of familiarity toward someone you assumed to be as sexually active and successful as yourself more annoying, but I couldn't. I loved it when you touched me, even if it was a different kind of affection than the one that I craved.

Once you'd left the bathroom, I locked the door behind you and stepped into the shower. As the hot water pattered down on my aching head, my mind burst with conflicting thoughts. Thoughts about you. I wanted to hate you so much for putting me through this chastening, humiliating experience. You had known exactly what you'd been doing. You had known what you'd been doing for you. You'd known what you'd been doing to me. You must have known. Or maybe you just ought to have known, but you really hadn't because you were thinking with your dick, not your brain. I was hurting for a number of reasons this morning, but the one that hurt the most was the sneaking suspicion that you really knew nothing about me that went beneath the obvious, the superficial. It once again made me question your judgment, and worse, it made me question mine. Your main objective for this sleepover had been to get laid, and in your defense, you probably thought you had been doing me a favor by setting me up like that and offering me an opportunity I had never asked for. You had handed me a freaking condom, and I'd taken it because I was hardwired to please you, to strive for your acclaim, your respect, the feeling of pride I felt when you were proud of me. Now you thought I'd had sex with Inka, and I couldn't bring myself to tell you the truth, because I didn't want to disappoint you. But why did I care so much about your feelings when you were so deliberately blind to mine? Maybe I didn't care so much about your feelings at all. Maybe I just cared about how your perception of me affected mine.

Closing my eyes, I propped my hands against the wall, bent my head under the shower head and let the water run down my back. In my mind, memories flashed up, images of you flipping burgers, topless and sweaty. Images of the tent you were sporting in your underpants when I'd seen you across the hall last night. Images of your junk as you stood next to me taking a leak. Images I hadn't even seen. You. Naked. In bed with Maia while I was dying a thousand little deaths in the room next door. Images I would never see. You and me together. Naked. Kissing. I felt a tingle in my groin. Hot water flowing on the outside, hot blood on the inside, my dick came to life, growing, pulsating in sync with my heartbeat. Pretending my hand was yours, I touched myself the way I wanted you to touch me, rough but loving, your clumsy brutality revealing your sexual inexperience. Boisterous, eager, clueless. Thinking of you, thinking of all the things I wanted you to do to me, all the things I wanted you to want me to do to you, I pleasured myself, indulged myself, aroused myself with the satisfaction of knowing how you would feel about the role you played in my dirty fantasies. You would have hated me if you'd known what I was doing, just like I hated you, knowing what you'd been doing in the room next door last night when you had abandoned me in an impossible situation that realistically had no other feasible outcome than my utter humiliation. Tightening my grip around my dick, I pretended my hand was your anus, and I thrust my pelvis forward, again and again, harder, faster, imagining your lustful moans, your restrained squeals as I made you walk that fine line between pleasure and pain the way you kept making me walk that line in our friendship. In my filthy mind I grabbed your hair and breathed down your neck, thrusting my pelvis harder against you, making you squeal louder as I was taming your convulsions with my body weight pressing down on you, not letting you escape, forcing you to endure my insatiable lust for you, my unappeasable love, my voracious desire to have you be mine and mine alone, my friend, my *boy*friend, my lover to have and to hold, to love and to cherish, for better, for worse, in sickness and in health until death do us part. A solitary tear, the love child of your agony and joy, escaped your eye and rolled down your face grimaced in pain, so I kissed it away. Your salty tear on my lips, your musky scent in my nose, I kept pushing, thrusting, forcing myself deeper and deeper into you until I eventually, finally, exploded into you as we became one for one fleeting, satisfying moment that would live forever tucked away in the back of my mind, for me to cherish forever in pleasure and in guilt, for you to never know because never know you must lest you hate me from the bottom of your heart until the end of your days.

EIGHT

I stared at the screen of my phone, and my heart skipped twenty beats. I didn't recognize the number, and I knew this couldn't be good. My phone knew the number of everyone who knew mine, or at least that's what I had thought until that morning when you pounced on me in school and scolded me for my precipitous departure right after breakfast on Sunday morning.

"Dude," you had said, "how could you be so stupid and run off without giving her your phone number?"

"I must have forgot," was the best response I could come up with, and it was another little white lie. The whole reason I left so early was because I didn't want to give Inka the time to ask for my number, because frankly, I had no intention to ever talk to her or look her in the eyes again. Not because she wasn't a nice person. She was. In fact, I really liked her, but that made it all the more difficult to brush off what had happened—or what hadn't happened, really—and not to be constantly reminded of the embarrassment and the humiliation whenever I thought of her. But I couldn't tell you that, obviously, because if I already felt embarrassed in front of Inka, how was I supposed to feel if you found out the truth? How were *you* supposed to feel? I thrived on your approval and your pride in me, and the thought of seeing disappointment in your eyes terrified me.

"Idiot," you said, punching my shoulder a little harder than necessary to prove your point. "But don't worry, I got your back. I gave her your number."

"That's great," I said, my voice devoid of any emotion as I tried to conceal my panic. "Thanks."

"You bet," you said, wrapping your arm around my neck, pulling me into a headlock and giving me a noogie. "Best friends forever, bro."

I couldn't even bring myself to fight back. I was already too busy trying to come up with an inconspicuous way to lose my phone, but in the end I had dismissed the idea and decided to face the inevitable like a man—a weak, terrified little man.

I tapped the green button and put the phone to my ear. "H-hello?"

"Tim?" Inka said, and I was surprised how easy it was to recognize a person's voice by a single uttered syllable even if you had never really heard that person talk all that much.

"Yes."

"Hi, it's Inka."

I cleared my throat and said, "Oh, hi." It was all I could come up with.

After an awkward pause, Inka said, "Tom gave me your number."

"Oh, okay. Sorry. I mean … yeah." I didn't even know why I was apologizing.

"So how are you holding up?"

She didn't waste any time and got straight to the point, and even though I knew feigning ignorance would only delay the inevitable, I said, "What do you mean?"

A longer pause. "I'm sorry I made you uncomfortable."

"What?" I said. "No, no. You … I mean, it's not your fault. It's … never mind."

"It is, though," she said. "I should have known better, but I got carried away."

I had no idea what she was talking about, and I was too scared to find out, so I didn't say anything.

"I thought you might want to talk."

Talk about what? About the most embarrassing night of my life? With the only person who was there to witness it? I'd rather have forgotten about it and never thought about it again for the rest of my life. "I don't know," I said.

"You don't know what?"

"I don't know what's there to talk about. I mean, what happened wasn't your fault, so … you know."

"I'm talking about your secret," she said.

I swallowed a huge lump in my throat. *My secret.* I only had one big secret that was worthy of the name, and I wondered how someone like Inka, whom I'd met only a few weeks ago, could possibly have any inkling what I'd been working so hard to keep from you for so long. I remembered all the times she had squinted at me with that subtle smile on her lips as if she'd been trying to see right through me. Maybe she hadn't just been trying.

My long silence prompted her to say, "It's okay, you don't have to say anything. This isn't a great conversation to have over the phone anyway, so I was thinking maybe you wanna grab a milkshake or something and we can talk?"

"Uh," I said, because really the answer was no, I did not wanna grab a milkshake and talk about my issues with her, but at the same time I knew I would have to because I needed to know what exactly she thought she knew, what she was planning to do with that information, and whether or not I might need to hire an assassin.

"Is that a yes?" she pressed me.

"I don't know, I guess?"

"Great. Tomorrow at four? At the Korova?" The smile in her voice had something endearing, but it was also a sign that maybe she hadn't really expected me to say yes.

"All right then."

"Okay," she said. "See you tomorrow."

"Okay." I put the phone down and threw myself on the bed. Hugging my pillow and closing my eyes, I tried to fend off a million thoughts that assaulted my mind. What was going on? What did Inka want from me? And how would it affect you and me? So many questions and no answers, just the daunting feeling that everything was about to change forever and that my life was never gonna be the same again. I was so scared.

* * *

"Why, hello there, pretty boy," Milo said, turning his head toward me as he operated the coffee machine. Wearing his white tank top, his suntanned skin glistening under the Korova's bright halogen lights. I wasn't thrilled to be announced to the moderately crowded place like that, but no one seemed to care except Inka who was sitting in our regular booth in the back, waving at me. "Your date is already here. So what's it gonna be, darling?"

It's not gonna be a date, I thought, but that was none of Milo's business, so I said, "That Double Dark Chocolate thing, please."

With a smile, Milo nodded. "Coming right up."

I made my way over to Inka and sat across the table from her.

"Hey," she said, still smiling.

"Hey."

"Thanks for coming."

I shrugged, not sure if I'd really had a choice. "I didn't have any other plans, so …"

"Right," she said. "No hanging out with Tom today?"

"Yeah, no. He's got soccer practice on Tuesdays."

"You're not into soccer?"

"I used to play," I said. "Same team as Tom, but I stopped when I entered high school. I still like watching it, though."

"He must have been disappointed."

Her remark struck me. It had never occurred to me before that you might have been disappointed when I quit playing soccer. If you had been, you had never let it on. I had stopped for a variety of reasons, not all of which I had wanted to share with you at the time. Like, for instance, the fact that since the onset of puberty I'd started feeling uncomfortable taking showers with you and the rest of the team. "I don't know," I said.

"I mean, you guys seem to do everything together. Almost like conjoined twins or something."

I squinted at her. "You mean like you and Maia?"

"Touché," she said and laughed.

"There you go, darling," Milo said, placing my milkshake in front of me. He looked at Inka. "Anything else for you?"

Her hand on her half-empty glass, she shook her head. "I'm good."

"All right," Milo said. "You guys need anything, you just holler."

As Milo made his way back behind the counter, Inka looked at me. "So how long have you known each other?"

"You mean Tom and I?"

She nodded.

"Since forever, really." I sucked on my straw to allow myself some time to decide if I should elaborate. "Since we were three or four, I think."

"Long time," Inka said. "And have you always been that close?"

"Of course."

"I'm just asking because I've known Maia almost as long as you've known Tom, but we only started hanging out and becoming friends a couple of years ago."

"Really?" I said, somewhat surprised. "What took you so long?"

She pondered the question for a moment, taking a swig from her milkshake. "I don't know. Circumstances? When you're a little kid, picking your friends isn't a rational decision. Heck, it's hardly even picking. You just take what's available. Sometimes it's a perfect match, sometimes not so much. Maia and I had different circles of friends when we were younger, so we never really had the chance to hang out and get to know each other. When we finally did, we immediately clicked in a way we'd never clicked with anyone else before. I mean, I can only speak for myself, but yeah."

Both hands on my glass, I stared at the millions of tiny little bubbles that constituted my milkshake, and I imagined that if I waited just long enough, even the last bubble would burst. It had never occurred to me that the one thing I valued the most in my life—my friendship with you—could have been nothing but the product of random chance, and I wondered what might have happened if we'd met later in life—or never at all, for that matter. If we hadn't known each other before and we'd met today, would we even have clicked? My heart said yes, we would always click because in a way we were made for each other, but my head was not so sure. I could take your taunting as playful or even affectionate banter because I knew you and I had known you almost my entire life. If we'd met today, your boisterous exuberance and rowdiness might have made me run for the hills and we might never even have gotten the chance to get to know each other. It was a disheartening thought.

"He doesn't know, does he?" Inka said, startling me out of my thoughts.

I raised my head. "Hm?"

"Tom. He doesn't know how you feel about him. I mean, how you *really* feel."

I looked at her. I looked for that subtle, almost taunting smile, that look in her eyes that almost gave away how she was able to see things most other people would never see, but there was no squint, no smile, just piercing green eyes that meant business. She knew. She'd always known, and now was the moment she wanted me to know. Whatever she wanted from me would be determined by my reaction. There was no point in lying to her.

Looking at my hands, I swallowed and shook my head. After a few moments of silence, I cast a cautious look at her to gauge her reaction. There was none, at least none that I could see. No smile, no understanding nod, nothing in her eyes that signaled approval or disapproval. She just looked at me as if she were waiting for me to elaborate, but what else was there to say, except …

"He must never know."

Finally, a twitching eyebrow, but still no response.

"It would destroy our friendship," I said in a low voice. "I can never let that happen. I mustn't."

She nodded. "I see."

"I mean, even if we were not ... both guys ... like, if he were a girl, I would never tell him—*her*—I'm in love with her if I hadn't received any previous signals that she might feel the same way about me. You know?"

"And you're one hundred percent sure he doesn't?"

I laughed out loud for a moment, then I turned serious again. "Trust me, Tom is the least gay person in the whole world. I've known him my entire life. There's absolutely no chance he's ... no. Just no. I mean, have you heard him talk about gay people?"

Inka took another swig from her milkshake. She put the glass back down and looked at me. "And you don't think he knows you just as well?"

I shook my head, and when I saw the look on Inka's face, I realized how this was an indictment of our friendship. It had always been clear to me that I knew you better than you knew me, but it had never bothered me or struck me as a problem. "Tom usually wears his heart on his sleeve. He says what he thinks and thinks what he says, you know?"

She chuckled. "It's pretty obvious. It's also pretty obvious you don't."

"I'm different," I said with a shrug. "I'm too self-conscious to let everyone inside my head."

"Fair enough, I guess. Anyway, I understand how you don't want him to know you're in love with him, especially if there's no chance he's gay himself. But what about coming out to him?"

I shook my head. "I don't know if I can do that."

"It's probably not gonna be easy," Inka said. "But you have to."

I frowned at her. "Why?"

"I mean, I can't tell you what to do, and I never would, because it's your decision, but don't you think he deserves to know?"

Avoiding her gaze, I swallowed. Trying hard not to burst into tears right in front of Inka, I slowly shook my head. "I don't know," I said in a low voice, my lips quivering. "I don't know how to tell him."

"Do you know anybody else who's gay?"

I kept shaking my head. "No. I don't know. No."

She sighed. "Oh well, I'm not exactly an expert on coming out either." After a pause, she added, "But I might know someone you could talk to."

I looked at her. "Who?"

"A friend of mine. Chris. He's gay and—"

"Oh, no." My shoulders slumping, I reclined against the backrest. "Please don't try to hook me up with some random gay dude."

Inka laughed out loud. "Oh, don't be silly, Tim. I'm not trying to hook you up. He's got a boyfriend. And besides, he's too old for you anyway."

"How old?"

"He's a freshman in college. He came out to his family and friends at fourteen and he's been openly gay ever since. I'm sure he can give you some good advice."

Rubbing my eyes, I sighed. "Oh, I don't know."

"Look, if you want to come out, you can either do it your own way, or you can get some advice first from someone who knows how it's done. It's not going to change the outcome, but it might make the process easier. The real question is, do you want to come out or not?"

I looked at her for a long time. She held my stare, that subtle smile back on her lips as if she already knew the answer. Deep down inside, I knew it too. It was like a dentist appointment you always knew was coming. You ignored it, putting your own mind at ease by pretending it wasn't going to happen, until one day your mom told you to brush your teeth and get in the car, and you suddenly realized there was no way to avoid the inevitable.

"So, um," I said, looking at my fingernails, "how would one get in touch with this … Chris? I mean, hypothetically."

With a smile, Inka picked up her phone. "Let me make a call."

NINE

I was sitting on a bench in the park, somewhere between the basketball courts and the baseball field. A bunch of high schoolers shooting hoops, a bunch of Little Leaguers doing batting practice, both groups coltish and loud, enjoying themselves, enjoying summer, enjoying their sense of belonging. I wanted to belong somewhere, too, although I wasn't exactly sure where.

Inka had wanted to set us up—me and that Chris guy—at the Korova, but I didn't feel comfortable with that idea. Going to a gay milk bar with you and the girls was one thing, going there without you was quite another. What if someone saw me there? Worse yet, what if by some freak coincidence *you* saw me there? With an openly gay guy three years my senior at that. There was no way I ever could have explained that away, and besides, meeting with Chris induced a feeling of claustrophobic anxiety in me that a confined space only would have exacerbated, so I had insisted on meeting him in an open, public space where I could pretend he and I were just accidentally walking next to each other in the same direction in case we met someone I knew. Or, should the need arise, I could just pick up my legs and run. Maybe I should have just got up and run before Chris was even here, because clearly, this was a stupid idea.

Someone was strutting toward me along the paved walkway. He was tall and handsome, with short, blond hair, but I wasn't sure if he looked anything like on the blurry photo Inka had shown me on her phone. Photo Chris had curly hair. This guy's hair was too short to tell if it would curl if he grew it. But he was the only person that had been walking in my direction since I had gotten here a quarter of an hour ago, and he was already running five minutes late, so who else would it be? As he approached me, I rubbed my sweaty palms on my jeans, wondering if I should remain seated or get up and walk toward him. What if it wasn't him after all? I didn't want to appear too eager, because I wasn't, but I didn't want to come off as standoffish either. Still walking in my direction, the guy was looking at his phone. Perhaps he was checking a photo of me Inka might have shared with him to make sure if I was me. Thirty feet away from me, he put his phone in his pocket. He was close enough now for me to notice a tattoo on his neck and another on his left arm. My heart sank because I found tattoos intimidating, and to be honest, from up close the guy didn't look gay at all, but what did I know? Maybe the secret to being out and proud was not looking like you were out and proud. At twenty feet, I rubbed my hands on my pants again, then I got up and walked toward him. My motion caught his attention and he looked me in the eyes, but there was no smile, no sign of recognition. Maybe the photo Inka had shown him was just as blurry as the photo of Chris she'd shared with me. At ten feet, my awkward smile was met by a frown, and he suddenly looked away, putting his hands in his pockets as he kept walking with no sign of slowing down. When he was right in front of me, I looked away too and put my hands in my pockets to keep them from shaking, my face flushing, my heart pounding like crazy, and I just kept walking past him, pretending to be in a hurry and going where I had meant to be going all along. I felt so awkward and embarrassed, I was seriously considering to just keep walking home.

"Hey!" I heard a voice behind me, and when I turned my head, there was a second guy, passing the first guy and walking in my direction. He, too, was tall and handsome and he did have blond, curly hair and the same bright smile like in the photo. "Tim?"

I stopped and turned around, taking my hands out of my pockets and putting them right back in. "Uh … yes."

As he jogged the last few steps toward me, his smile grew brighter, brighter even than the tie-dyed, rainbow-colored letters on his white T-shirt spelling out the word *Pride*, and I wondered if meeting with him in public where everyone could see us had really been such a great idea. He stopped in front of me, still smiling, his blue eyes sparkling like the ocean on a sunny summer day. As I offered my hand for him to shake, he raised both his arms, ready for a hug. I didn't know that I was ready to hug a gay stranger in a park, but I withdrew my hand and raised my arms. At the same time, he lowered his arms and extended his hand. This was awkward and silly, and we both knew it, so we laughed.

"Come here, you," he finally said, raising his arms again, and I leaned forward, reluctantly, making sure our bottom halves didn't touch, because I was worried my body might be more excited about this unexpected closeness than I was, and ready to show it, too. While he rubbed my back, I patted his twice. Then we parted again, the scent of his sweet cologne lingering in my nose. "Sorry I'm late. Had a hard time finding a parking space."

"Oh, okay. Sorry about that," I said as if it was my fault, which it probably was because I had picked the location and there was a parking lot right next to the Korova.

"I hope I didn't make you wait too long."

I shook my head and waved my hand. "Nah, it's okay. I literally just got here." It was literally a lie, but I didn't want to make him feel bad, because now that the first awkwardness was subsiding, I found myself to kind of like the guy.

"Good." He looked around. "You want to go somewhere or …"

I looked around, too, as if the swings and slides were an actual option. "Yeah, no, I don't know. Maybe let's just take a walk?"

"Sure," he says.

We walked in silence for a few moments as I tried to come up with a way to get to the point without seeming too eager, too desperate.

"So—"

"Well, first of all thank you for agreeing to see me," I interrupted him. "I know this is weird and awkward and whatnot."

Too shy to look at him directly, I saw him shaking his head from the corner of my eye.

"Not at all," he said. "Inka told me about your situation."

"Oh yeah? So, what did she tell you exactly?"

"That you have a crush on your best friend."

"Who's a boy," I said, "who's totally not gay."

"Right."

"But that's not really the problem."

Chris looked at me. "Oh? It's not?"

"No, I mean, of course it's a problem, like every time someone's got a crush on someone who will never love them back. I assume that in the history of mankind this may have happened before."

"Once or twice," Chris said.

"Right, so that's kind of a normal problem, and there's no point trying to solve it because there is no solution. Tom isn't gay and that's never gonna change."

"Are you sure about that?"

I looked at him. "About what? That he's not gay or that he never will be?"

"How about both?"

"Honestly," I said, "Tom is the least gay person I know. And also the last person I can see doing something crazy like, you know, trying to explore something different in a moment of weakness, like when he's drunk or something."

"Mh-hm. And I'm sure he'd say the same thing about you."

"I don't know. Probably. Maybe. I'm not sure."

He looked at me with a subtle smile that rivaled Inka's. "Except he'd be totally wrong about that, wouldn't he?"

I knew what he was getting at, but I had no response, so I exhaled.

"You know what I mean?" Chris said. "I mean, I don't want to get your hopes up or make up a problem where you say there is none. All I'm saying is you can see only this far." He tapped his finger on his forehead. "Everything that's going on behind here you can never really know."

I shook my head. "Yeah, no, not Tom though. Nothing gay about him. In fact, I think he hates gays."

"Why would you think that?"

"Well, the way he talks about them. Calling them fags and things like that."

"Oh," Chris said. "Well, that sucks."

"Yeah."

"Still doesn't mean anything, though. I'm speaking from experience."

I cast a frown at him. "You call gay people fags too?"

He laughed. "No! But I know someone. A friend of mine, Jack. He's been known to bully gay kids in school and call them worse things than just fags."

"But he's really gay? Is that what you're saying?"

Chris shook his head. "He'd kill me if I went around telling people he's gay. In his opinion, homosexuality is a perversion. He just happens to enjoy engaging in perverted sex practices. Occasionally. Mostly when he's drunk."

"Wow."

"I know, right? Some people have a hard time coming to terms with their own sexuality. There used to be a lot more people like this, back when queer people weren't as widely accepted as they are now, but they do still exist. And some people like to call out other people on their supposed flaws to distract from their own. I'm not saying I like it, but who am I to judge? Personally, I think he'd be happier if he accepted himself the way he is and didn't care so much about what other people might think of him, but you can't force people to be happy if they prefer to be miserable."

I pondered his words, my hands deep in my pockets. As much as I would have liked to believe you might secretly be gay, I just couldn't. This was not you, and to be perfectly honest, I didn't even want it to be you. I didn't want you to be miserable and in self-denial. I wanted you to be you, and I wanted you to want me to be me. Was I asking for too much? I looked at Chris. "So, how did you find out?"

"That Jack's a perverted heterosexual?"

I laughed. "Yeah."

"My gaydar is pretty reliable. I'm not easy to fool. So I got him drunk, showed him some gay porn, and when I saw the bulge in his pants, I made my move."

"Wow," I said.

"The next day at school, he told me that whatever had happened between us was a one-time thing. An experiment. One that would never happen again. The day after that, he showed up at my place, unannounced and with a backpack full of beer."

"For more experiments?"

Chris chuckles. "Yeah."

"So are you guys still … I mean …"

"Oh, no, no." He shook his head. "We did that for a couple of months, but I had to end it. I can't live like that, hiding who I am or who I'm on love with, going to the Pride parade alone while my boyfriend is sitting at home in his closet. So, as a couple, we never had a future. We're still friends, though."

"Right," I said, wondering however that might work.

He suddenly made a quick move, threw his body in front of mine and caught a rogue soccer ball that was heading straight for my face.

"Sorry!" someone called over from the soccer field.

Chris dropped the ball, did a couple of kick-ups with both his feet, a little higher each time until he finally gave it a powerful kick and sent it back straight into the arms of that soccer player a hundred feet away. I'd be lying if I said his athletic prowess wasn't a huge turn on.

"Thank you!" the soccer player said with a wave of his hand, and we kept on walking, Chris on my other side now.

"So, what does your gaydar say about me?" I said.

He grinned at me. "Well, I already knew you were gay before I got here, but …" He eyed me up and down, crumpled his nose, nodded and said, "Yeah."

My face flushed, and Chris laughed.

"Don't worry. My gaydar is very finely tuned. You being gay is probably not the first thing people think about you when they see you."

"Jeez, thanks, I guess."

"Which, ironically, might make things more difficult."

I cast him a questioning look. "Why?"

"There was this other guy I knew in high school who also had a hard time coming out, but when he finally did, everyone was like, 'Yeah, what else is new?' You know what I mean?"

"I guess," I say. "So was it like that for you too? I mean, when you came out?"

"Kind of. I never really tried to hide who I am, so when I came out to my friends and family, no one was really all that surprised. Well, except my grandma, but she's completely clueless when it comes to gender issues. She actually burst into tears because she thought being gay meant I was going to grow boobs and get gender reassignment surgery."

"Ouch."

"I know, right?" We reached a bench at the end of the soccer field, and Chris nudged me with his elbow. "Wanna sit for a minute?"

I shrugged. "Sure."

As I sat down, Chris pulled a pack of cigarettes out of his pocket and offered it to me.

"No, thanks," I said, shaking my head.

He put a cigarette in his mouth, lit it, and sat down next to me, placing the cigarettes and lighter between us on the bench. "So, what about your parents?"

"My parents aren't gay either, I don't think."

Chris laughed out loud.

"Seriously, though," I said, "what about them?"

"Would they be surprised to find out you're gay? Or how do you think they'd take it?"

I gazed across the soccer field. At the other end, someone scored a goal, and his team mates quickly surrounded him, hugging him, ruffling his hair and slapping his butt. Maybe I should have just kept playing soccer so I could have hugged you and slapped your butt whenever you scored a goal, and no one, not even you, ever would have thought it was weird or inappropriate. "Probably not," I said. "My mom will cry her heart out because she can't have grandkids, and my dad will finally get why I can't throw a baseball to save my life, but I don't think they'll be mad and disown me or anything."

Chris took a long drag on his cigarette and nodded. "I like how you say 'will,' not 'would.' I think deep down inside you're ready to come out, even if you may not feel like it."

"Yeah, well, my parents are not who I'm worried about."

"I know, it's Tom," Chris said, smoke coming out of his nose and mouth as he spoke.

I nodded.

"But you do want to come out to him, don't you?"

I watched the soccer game in silence for a long while. Having thought about this question for months, I should have had an answer ready by now, but I didn't.

"I take that as a 'I don't know,'" Chris finally said.

I looked at him, shrugging and nodding at the same time.

"Okay, then let's break it down," he said. He took another drag on his cigarette. "Picture this: you meet someone. Sweetest, sexiest, most handsome guy you've ever met. You fall in love, and he falls right back in love with you, and you realize that loving him and being loved back is the greatest and most satisfying feeling in the world. You still following?"

"Sure," I said, smiling because the picture he painted was so intriguing.

"You want to keep that from your best friend? Your relationship, your happiness, everything? How is that supposed to work?"

The smile on my lips died a quick death. On the surface, what Chris said didn't even make any sense. How could I ever fall in love with someone else as long as I was in love with you? The thought of spending my life with someone else had never even occurred to me. Sex, yes. Quick, secret, dirty sex with someone who liked it and who wouldn't expect or ask for anything more. But a relationship that would blossom into a lifelong bond, loving, caring, inseparable, with someone who was not you was something I had never even tried to imagine. All my visions of the future revolved around you and me and an eclectic cast of supporting characters, none of which would ever get between us and our friendship. It was a vision that was pure, innocent, and … infantile. It was like a four-year-old who was dead set on marrying his mom. It was never going to happen. Somewhere deep down inside I must have always known that the fairy tale I'd been telling myself in a hidden crevice of my mind was just that: a fairy tale. A fairy tale that, like most fairy tales, would never come true.

I shook my head. "I don't know."

"It's not gonna work," Chris said. "Your guilt will eat away at your happiness, and you'll live in constant fear that Tom will somehow find out, and through some freak coincidence he probably will."

"Right," I said, my heart sinking.

"Trust me, don't underestimate freak coincidences. Sooner or later something stupid will happen, and then how are you gonna explain to your best friend that you lied to him all this time?"

I rubbed my eyes because the thought made my tear ducts ready to burst. "Shit."

"You have to tell him. Or remain a virgin forever. You want to remain a virgin forever, Tim?"

I scoffed. "No?"

"Good boy, because that would be such a waste."

"But what if … what if he doesn't take it well? What if he hates me? What if he tells me to go to hell and—"

"Tim? Tim! Listen to me," Chris interrupted me, putting his hand on my shoulder and waiting for me to turn my head and look at him. "No offense, and you're not gonna like this, but you need to understand something. Anyone who hates you for being gay is *not* your friend." He glared at me, no trace of a smile left on his face, and as he squeezed my shoulder to underline his point, I started welling up. The insinuation that you might not be the friend I had always thought you were, that under the right or wrong circumstances you might not have my back, that you might abandon me and everything we had was such a painful sting to my heart that I could hardly hold back my tears.

"I'm so scared," I said with quivering lips like a little girl who just found out Santa isn't real.

"I understand that," Chris said, squeezing my shoulder harder, "but you see, it is what it is, even if you don't even know what it is yet. If—*when*—he finds out, he will have to make a decision. You can't take that away from him, nor should you. He may support you or he may not support you. If he's the friend you think he is, he will support you, but either way, you have to give him the chance to make that decision. Otherwise it wouldn't be fair. Not fair to him and not fair to yourself."

Wiping my snotty nose with the back of my hand, I slowly nodded. I know he was right. I'd always known I would have to tell you one day, I just kept putting it off because I didn't know how.

"Fuck," I said in a low voice.

"That's the spirit," he said, letting go of my shoulder and patting my back.

"So how am I gonna do it?"

Chris took a last drag on his cigarette, dropped it on the ground and stomped it out with his foot. He turned his head away to exhale the smoke, then he looked back at me. "There are a million ways to come out, and all of them don't work for everyone. There is no magic formula."

"That's helpful."

Ignoring the snark in my voice, Chris said, "I guess the most common way is to just wait for the right moment and have the talk. Just say, 'Hey, by the way, I'm gay and I thought you should know,' and then take it from there. Or, if you're scared of his reaction, you could have other people around. Like Inka and Maia. Or some of your other friends. The problem with making a big announcement to the masses is that you might make it a bigger issue than you want to."

I raised my eyebrows at him. "But that's what you did, isn't it?"

"Yes, and that's why I know what I'm talking about. A person's sexual orientation shouldn't even be an issue at all, so why turn it into an issue yourself?"

"That's what I'm asking you," I said. "Why *did* you do it then?"

He grinned. "Because I was young and stupid and I didn't know any better. Now I do, and I wouldn't do it again. I don't owe anybody an explanation of who I am."

"Wait," I said, "I'm confused. You just said not telling Tom wouldn't be fair. Now you say I don't owe him an explanation."

"You owe him the truth," Chris said. "But you don't have to explain yourself to him or anyone else. It's not like sexual orientation is a choice. You are who you are, whether anyone likes it or not. Whether *you* like it or not."

Looking at the sky, squinting against the sun, I exhaled. There was no easy solution to this. But there were some solutions that seemed easier than others. I just had to figure out what would work best for me. For us. "Okay," I finally said.

"Okay?"

"Yeah."

"What does that mean? Okay what?"

I scratched my head sheepishly. "I have no fucking idea. I don't want to sit down with him and have 'the talk.' Or with anyone else for that matter. I like the idea of just trying to be myself and stop hiding, though."

"Good," Chris said. "Then that's what you're gonna do. Just be yourself. If you see someone cute on the street, don't pretend you don't want to look. Find gay friends. Belt out show tunes in public. Don't come out, be out, and ride that rainbow."

I laughed. "Right. Not sure if anyone would want to hear me sing or where to find gay friends, but okay."

"You seem nice enough," he said, "so we can be friends. That would be a start." When he saw the look on my face, he laughed out loud. "Don't worry, I'm not hitting on you. I have a boyfriend, and I'm actually very faithful."

"Right, okay," I said because I didn't know what else to say. He was so sweet and kind, I would have loved to be friends with him, but things were suddenly moving so fast and they kept picking up speed. It was dizzying.

"Tell you what," he said, "why don't you join me and Sam and Jack this weekend? We're going to the Unicorn Club on Friday."

"What's that?"

"A dance club. Well, a gay dance club. It's down in Santa Ana."

I shook my head emphatically. "Yeah, thanks, but no. I got zero chance of getting into a club. I mean, look at me. I'm sixteen, looking twelve."

Chris smiled. "Once a month they have an event called *Sparkles*. It's for teens aged fourteen to nineteen. Because, you know, baby unicorns are called sparkles. Anyway, Sam is actually twenty, but he's got a fake ID that says he's eighteen."

"I never heard of someone getting a fake ID so they can pass as younger than they actually are."

"He specifically got it for *Sparkles*, because it's such a fun event. We go there every month. You're welcome to tag along."

"Oh, I don't know," I said, but deep down inside I did, really.

He nudged me with his elbow. "It's gonna be fun."

I looked at him, at his bright smile and his sparkling blue eyes, almost envious of his self-confidence, his poise, his self-acceptance. The thought that one day I could have all that myself forced a longing smile on my face.

"You know you want it," he teased me.

Covering my head with both arms, I groaned. "I can't believe I'm going to a gay club!"

"That's the spirit!" Chris said, ruffling my hair. "I knew it! You're gonna love it, I promise."

His heartfelt enthusiasm was contagious, and I was overcome by an immense sense of pride and accomplishment. I was taking an invisible first step, and while it may seem like a small step to you, for me it was a giant leap that required an amount of courage that I had always hoped to muster one day but never quite believed I ever could.

We finished our walk, and on our way to his car, Chris offered me a ride home, but I shook my head. "Thanks, but it's just a short walk home for me, and I need a little time to let everything sink in."

"I understand," Chris said.

We left the park, and as we were about to cross the street, I heard an all familiar voice behind us. "Hey!"

We both turned our heads, and my face flushed when I saw you and Maia, hand in hand, strolling in our direction.

"Oh, hey," Chris said, and I was momentarily confused until I realized he wasn't responding to you but greeting Maia. She was Inka's best friend, so of course Chris knew her too.

As Chris hugged Maia, you and I exchanged our regular bro handshake, but there was nothing regular about the look in your eyes. Bewildered and irritated, your piercing eyes demanded answers to unasked questions. I felt queasy, almost nauseous, like I had on that suspension bridge in Sequoia back when we were twelve and you rocked the bridge, knowing it would freak me out. I remember the glee in your eyes as I held on to the ropes, scared of falling into the river below. There was no glee in your eyes today, but I felt queasy just the same, as if I was about to fall into an abyss.

Chris and Maia ended their hug and we all stood there in awkward silence for a few moments.

"Well?" you finally said looking at me.

"Oh, uh," I said, gesturing back and forth between you and Chris. "Chris, this is Tom. Tom, this is Chris. He's a friend of Inka's."

"Right," you said and extended your hand, briefly looking Chris in the eyes before your gaze wandered down to the rainbow-colored *Pride* on his T-shirt. Chris shook your hand. It was an awkward, business-like handshake, and I felt as if I were at a dinner party introducing my old boss to my new one.

"Nice to meet you," Chris said. He turned to Maia. "What are you guys doing here?"

"Nothing, just going for a walk," Maia said.

"Yeah, us too," I volunteered, and I immediately regretted making it sound as if my budding friendship with the relative stranger Chris still was remotely resembled yours with your girlfriend. "I mean … you know."

"Uh huh."

"Anyway, we were just about to go home. I mean, I'm going home. Not sure where he's going."

Chris looked at his watch and said, "Actually, I have to pick up Sam from work, so I better get going."

I was grateful he refrained from mentioning that Sam was his boyfriend, but the feeling of relief didn't last long, because after hugging Maia good bye, he turned to me to do the same, and I was too flabbergasted to turn around and run into the moving traffic.

"Oh, a hug. Okay then," I said as he wrapped his arms around me and rubs my back. It lasted just a second, but your glare made it feel like an hour, and when he finally released me, he said, "I'll call you about Friday."

I wanted to hate him, not just for the hug but especially for mentioning Friday, which didn't do anything to thaw your icy glare, but I had to give it to him, he didn't mess around, and I probably couldn't expect him to lie for me.

"All right," I mumbled, and as he crossed the street, I turned to you and Maia. "Well, I gotta run. Can't be late for dinner."

Still glaring at me, you said, "It's four o'clock."

"Yeah, no, I know. Uh, we're having a barbecue. Dad wants to start early, in case it starts to rain later."

There wasn't a cloud in the sky.

"Right, whatever."

After a bro shake with you and a hug with Maia, I turned around and walked away, and I kept feeling your glare on the back of my neck until I turned the next corner.

* * *

When I strolled into the kitchen, Dad was sitting at the counter, hammering away at his laptop.

"Hey, Dad," I said as I headed for the fridge.

"Oh, hey, buddy," he said, his eyes glued to the screen.

I grabbed the orange juice from the fridge, leaned against the counter top, and started drinking right from the carton.

"Mind using a glass?"

I shook my head. "Almost empty. I'll finish it."

Dad didn't respond, granting me this small victory. As I kept taking little swigs from the carton, I cast furtive glances at him until he finally took his eyes off the screen and looked at me over the rim of his glasses. "Everything all right?"

"Can I ask you something?" I said.

"Sure, ask away."

"Why do you always write in the kitchen?"

He looked at me for a long while, waiting for me to take another swig until he finally said, "It's where the fridge is."

I quickly lowered the carton and covered my mouth and nose with my other hand, but it was too late. My nose was already spewing orange juice across the floor. As Dad looked back at the screen, shaking his head, I put the carton on the counter and got a rag from the sink. Getting down on my knees to clean up the mess, I said, "Dad?"

"Hm?"

"Do you ever write any gay characters?"

There was no response until I took the rag back to the sink and saw him staring at me. "Georgiana Tinderbottom's assistant, Dick Cummings, is gay. Why?"

"Just curious," I said, making my way back to the counter and picking up the juice carton. "So, how do you know how to write gay people when you're not, you know, gay yourself?"

"Same way I write murderers without ever actually having killed someone. By keeping my eyes open and being a keen observer. By the time you've reached my age, you'll probably have met a gay person or two." He was still staring at me, gauging my reaction.

"Yeah, I guess." I took another swig of juice, emptying the carton. Screwing the cap back on, I said, "I'm going to a gay club on Friday."

Suddenly sitting up straight, he took off his glasses. "Are you now?"

"Yep."

His eyes followed me around the kitchen as I took the empty juice carton to the trashcan and headed for the door. "Anyway, gonna take a shower. See ya."

"Whoa, whoa, wait, hang on," I heard him say behind me. "Get back here a minute."

I turned around and made my way back to the counter. Avoiding my dad's gaze, I picked up a rubber band from the counter and started playing with it to keep my hands from shaking.

"Look at me, Tim."

Without raising my head, I looked at him.

"Anything you want to tell me?"

I shrugged. This was not going the way I had always imagined my coming out would go one day, and I blamed Chris. In a good way. I'd never been good at taking control of a conversation. I felt more comfortable when I could just respond, especially if I could anticipate the questions. "I don't know," I said. "Anything you wanna know?"

"Yes," he said, "I want to know *everything*."

"It's an event for teens fourteen to nineteen. They don't serve booze, and it ends at ten."

Dad nodded. "Right. And you want to go because …?"

"A friend of mine is going, and he invited me to tag along."

"What friend?"

"Chris. You don't know him. He's a friend of Tom's girl-friend's best friend."

"And you like him."

"Yeah," I said. Then I realized Dad probably had a more specific definition of the word 'like' in mind, so I quickly added, "I mean, not like that. Not romantically or anything. Besides, he's got a boyfriend anyway, so …"

"Right." He looked at me for a long time, and I assumed he needed that time to muster the courage for his next question. "So, you're not gay?"

"I didn't say that."

There was another long pause before he said, "Are you gay?"

By now I'd had enough time to prepare for the inevitable question, so I didn't hesitate to say, "Yes." The hard part was holding Dad's stare, but I somehow managed. He looked at me with no discernible reaction on his face until he finally said, "Oh, okay," and focused his attention back on the screen of his laptop. I was about to turn around and leave when he said, "Does your mother know?"

"Nope."

The shadow of a smile crossed his lips. My parents usually didn't compete for my affection, but I could tell he was pleased I had let him know first.

"You want me to tell her?" he asked. His question made me feel all warm and fuzzy inside, and I was tempted to ask him if he could not only tell Mom but you as well, but I guess that would have been asking for too much.

"Would you?" I said.

His smile grew brighter, warmer, and he said, "Sure." The he got up, wrapped his arms around me and gave me a tight hug. "I love you, buddy."

"I love you too, Dad," I said, and I had no time to burst into tears because the front door opened and Mom came in, carrying two lucky bamboo plants.

"Look what I got!" she said, but when she saw us, still hugging, her expression changed from proud shopper to suspicious mother. "What's going on?"

"Guess what," Dad said, ending our embrace but keeping his arm around my shoulder. "Our son is going to a dance."

Mom put the plants on the counter. "Oh, that's nice. What kind of dance?"

"Long story," Dad said. "I'll tell you in a minute." He pushed me away. "You go and take your shower already. You reek like a locker room."

"Yes, Dad," I said and ran for the hills.

TEN

"So, how did your mom take it?" Chris asked, looking at me over his shoulder. He was riding shotgun in his boyfriend's Camry. Sam was driving. I had only met him a few minutes ago, but I had already taken to him. He was the kind of guy no one needed a gaydar for, and he'd had me at 'Hello.'

Rolling my eyes, I groaned. It was a slightly theatrical groan, the kind I never would have done in front of you because it would have raised your eyebrows and made you look at me funny. But I had never been surrounded by so many exclusively gay people, so I felt all gay and jaunty myself. "Don't get me started," I said. "It was such a cryfest. She burst into my room, threw herself around my neck and cried her heart out." I probably wouldn't have told you that kind of thing either, because rather than making fun of my mom, you would have ridiculed me for being a mama's boy.

"That sounds just like *my* mom," Sam said, pulling up at a stop sign, looking left and right.

"Seriously," I said, "it was as if my dad had told her I was joining a cult or something."

"But you are, darling," Sam said. "Today you're joining the most fabulous cult ever, and you'll never look back."

Chris Laughed. "Stop scaring him!"

"Hey, I'm just saying."

Turning back to me, Chris said, "Don't worry, she'll get over it."

"Yeah, no, she's fine. Deep down inside she already knew, she said. But remember how I told you she'd be upset about not having grandkids?"

"Yeah."

"That's exactly what she said." I mimicked her crying voice. "'I'll never have grandkids!'"

Chris shrugged. "Ah well, you can always adopt."

"That's what *I* said. And then she cried even harder."

"So, what about Tom?"

"Who's Tom?" Sam said.

"Tim's homophobic best friend," Chris replied, and my heart sank a little. I still didn't want to believe you were as homophobic as you often appeared to be. I liked to think your remarks were just fueled by careless ignorance and once you realized your best friend is gay, you'd change your perspective.

"Tom definitely knows something's going on. Yesterday he asked me if I was coming to his soccer game tonight. He never does that. He plays every Friday night. Sometimes I come to watch him play, sometimes I don't. But he never asks."

"We come every Friday night, don't we?" Sam said, looking at Chris.

Chris slapped his shoulder and turned to me. "So, what did you say?"

"Well, I didn't tell him I'm going to a gay club, if that's what you're asking. I kinda dodged the question. I said we'll see.

Didn't want to lie to him, so I didn't say yes. Didn't say no because then he would have asked me why not and if I had anything else planned. What was I supposed to say to that?"

"How about the truth?"

I shook my head. "Didn't feel like the right moment, I don't know." Chris didn't reply, so after a few moments of silence, I added, "I know, I'm a wuss."

"Don't say that," Chris reprimanded me without looking at me. "No one expects you to go from zero to sixty in three seconds. As long as you're determined to get there it's okay to take your time."

"Amen," Sam said. Then the two look at each other and said in unison, "Gay men!"

"I am," I said, but it was more self-encouragement than a declaration of intent. Right now, my strategy was to keep telling myself I was ready until I actually believe it.

We pulled into the parking lot of a strip mall. A dentist, a laundromat, a 7-Eleven and a Mexican fast food joint. I had lived in Brookhurst my entire life, but there were still areas I'd literally never been to. While far from desolate, this place looked distinctly more run-down than I was used to, and there was a sign in the window of the 7-Eleven that read *Liquor Available Here!* We didn't have that at the 7-Eleven around the corner from where I lived.

"There he is," Chris said.

Right under the booze sign, between the garbage can and the entrance, a guy of Chris and Sam's age was sitting on the ground, eating a burrito. He was wearing black sneakers, blue jeans, and a denim jacket over a gray hoodie. His ash blond hair was cropped short but still long enough to look messy. Blinded by our headlights, he looked up as we pulled into the parking space right in front of him.

"I swear to God," Sam said, "if he farts inside the car again, I'm gonna kill him. This time, I'm gonna kill him."

Jack put his hand on the garbage can to pull himself up, taking another bite from the burrito in his other hand. He walked around the car and opened the passenger-side back door.

"No food in the car!" Sam shouted over his shoulder.

"Fucking hell!" Jack slammed the door shut again. On his way back to the garbage can, he stuffed the rest of the burrito in his mouth before he disposed of the tinfoil wrapper. Wiping his hands on his jeans, he made his way back to the car door, opened it and slid into the seat next to me. He fist-bumped Chris and Sam and said, "Whaddup, hoes?" Then he turned to me. "Who the hell are you?"

"Uh, Tim," I said, raising my fist for a fist bump.

Ignoring the fist, he said, "You a fag like these two, Uh-Tim?"

"I really wish you'd stop calling people fags all the time," Sam said, putting the car in reverse and pulling out of the parking space.

"And I want a million dollars," Jack said. "Now what?"

"Tom does that, too," I said.

"Yeah, well," Chris said, and I wasn't sure if he was talking to Sam or me. "Some people struggle with their own sexual identity so much, they have to compensate by calling other people names. Right, Jack?"

"Yeah, fuck you too," Jack said, but there was no venom in his voice. It almost sounds affectionate. He looked at me again. "What are you, like, twelve? Will I go to jail when I touch your junk?"

"I'm sixteen."

"It's *if*, not *when*, Jack," Chris said. "And you're not gonna touch his junk, or I will chop off yours with a hedge trimmer."

"All right, all right, I was just checking," Jack said. He finally offered me his fist. "Jack."

I bumped it. "Nice to meet you."

"Yeah, whatever."

Sam looked at Jack in the rear view mirror. "Buckle up, Jack."

"Yes, ma'am!" Jack said, grabbing his seat belt.

We pulled out of the parking lot and merged into the southbound rush hour traffic on Harbor Boulevard. The sun would still be up for half an hour, but it was hidden somewhere behind a rare, thick layer of clouds, so cars and roadside businesses had turned their lights on. I loved driving at dusk, surfing a sea of lights that provided orientation and comfort, no matter how dark the coming night was going to be.

"So who's your boyfriend?" I heard Jack say, and it wasn't until I turned my head and looked at him that I realized he was talking to me.

"Uh, I don't have a boyfriend."

He continued looking at me with a blank look on his face, as if he was taking his time to process what I said, then he said, "What about that Tom guy?"

"Oh," I say, shaking my head, "no, no. He's not my boyfriend. He's just a friend. My best friend, actually."

"Best friend, huh?" Jack said. "He a fag too?"

"Nope. Straight as an arrow."

Jack took his time again to respond. "But he knows you're gay, right?"

"No."

"No? What do you mean, no?"

"I mean, not yet."

He looked puzzled. "How can he be your best friend and not know you're gay?"

"Jack," Chris chipped in, "take it easy, okay?"

109

Kicking the seat in front of him, Jack said, "Shut up, bitch, I'm just asking a question."

"Dude," Sam said, glaring at Jack over his shoulder, "can you not kick the seat with your filthy feet?"

"Can you guys get off my back? I'm trying to have a conversation!" He turned back to me. "Seriously, how can he be your best friend and not know you're gay?"

"I don't know," I said. "I haven't found the right moment to tell him yet."

"No, I mean … why do you even have to tell him? He should know. What kind of a best friend is he if he doesn't know shit about you?"

"Um, broken gaydar?" I said with an awkward grin.

Jack shook his head. "Fucking hell."

"Same reason most people don't know you're gay, Jack."

"Fuck you," Jack said. "And FYI, I'm not gay. I'm bisexual. Ninety-five percent hetero. It's just that most girls are fucking princesses who want you to drive them around all day and expect you to buy them flowers and pay for their food and movie tickets and shit. Like, who do they think I am, Jeb Bozos or something? Bitch, you want flowers, try your luck at the gas station down the street. Do I look like a florist? And when you burp or fart or something, they act like you just strangled a kitten. Ain't gonna put up with that kind of shit just to have a trench I can lay my pipe in."

"At least that's what he keeps telling himself," Chris said.

Jack leaned forward, rested his chin on the backrest of Chris's seat and tapped him on the shoulder. When Chris turned his head to the side, Jack discharged a ginormous burp right into his face. The burp wasn't even going in my direction, but the pungent stench of half-digested burrito and gastric acid immediately flooded the inside of the car.

"Oh, for the love of God!" Chris said, holding his nose and turning his head the other way.

Sam pressed the button to lower his window. "You are so fucking disgusting, Jack! Cursed be the day my parents taught me that violence is not a solution."

Jack looked at me and shrugged. "See? Like I said: girls."

Without passing any judgment one way or the other, I found myself smiling at him because his attitude had a certain charm. He just didn't give a shit, and while I had no intentions to become a rude, obnoxious misogynist who burped in people's faces, I did envy his ability to unapologetically be himself. I couldn't help but wonder, though, why this ability didn't extend to his sexuality. If Chris was right about Jack being gay, that is.

"Anyway," Jack said, "you have to tell him. That friend of yours. That Ted guy."

"Tom."

He frowned. "I thought you were Uh-Tom."

"No, I'm Tim."

"Right, whatever. Just tell him, and if he's got a problem with it, tell him he's an idiot for not noticing."

"Do I look that gay then?" I asked.

"Hell yeah." He reached into the inside pocket of his jacket, pulling out a small vodka bottle. The sound of him unscrewing the cap prompted Sam to turn around.

"Is that what I think it is?"

Jack shakes his head. "No, you pervert! It's just vodka." He took a swig and sloshed it around in his mouth like mouthwash before he swallowed it.

"Great," Sam said. "Gonna be lit if the cops pull us over and the whole car reeks of booze."

"To be perfectly honest," Chris said, "it's better than that burrito smell."

Jack nudged me with his knee and offered me the bottle.

"Uh, no thanks," I said, shaking my head. "I'm only twelve."

It wasn't really that funny, but Jack burst out laughing, putting his soft, warm hand in my neck. "I like you, Uh-Tim. You're funny. Not like these two butt munchers here."

The expression 'butt munchers' made me chuckle, which was probably extremely politically incorrect, but I couldn't help it.

"Look at these two," Chris said to Sam. "Looks like somebody found a new friend."

I wasn't sure if he was talking about me or Jack, so I asked, "Are you talking about me?"

Chris looked at me over his shoulder and winked. "I don't know, am I?"

Smiling back at him, I said, "I don't know."

ELEVEN

The air inside the Unicorn Club was hot and humid and throbbing with the rhythm of deafening electro-pop beats. Laser beams cut through artificial fog, and there was a pervasive waft lingering everywhere, a mixture of sweat, cologne, and energy drinks. Or maybe that was just me, because back home I had put on half a bottle of cologne, I was on my second energy drink, and I was sweating like a pig. Clasping my Monster Energy can with both hands, I was leaning on the railing of a sixty-foot long balcony overlooking the dance floor. Below me, some five or six hundred teens were moving to the music, having a great time just being themselves. Not all of them were gay. I saw plenty of straight couples kissing, dancing, and talking to their gay friends. It fueled my envy, not merely their ability to attend a gay club and enjoying themselves like it was nobody's business, but doing so with their straight friends. I wondered if you would ever find it in your heart to come here with me and be a part of my world the way I had always been a part of yours. It pained me that deep down inside, I already seemed to know the answer, and what scared me the most was that if we started living in separate worlds, we'd create a rift between us that would grow, perhaps very slowly at first, but it would continue to grow and keep driving us further and further apart. I didn't want that. But I didn't want to keep lying to you either. I wanted to stop hiding who I was, and I wanted to become a part of that new world I was taking my first unsteady steps into tonight. It was a strange world, confusing and scary, but it was also bright and colorful and enticing. I saw guys kissing guys and girls kissing girls, and no one gave a damn. It felt right. It felt like I belonged in this world, much more so than I belonged on a double date with you and the girls.

Someone tapped me on my right shoulder, and when I turned my head, there was no one there, at least no one I knew, so I turned my head to the left and looked into Chris's grinning face.

"What are you doing up here?" he shouted over the music.

I shook my head. "Nothing. Just taking in the view."

"You should be down there enjoying yourself."

"Nah, I'm good. I feel stupid standing on the dance floor watching other people dance."

"You're not supposed to watch other people dance," Chris said. "You're supposed to dance."

"I'm not much of a dancer."

"Says who?"

"Says I."

"What do *you* know? Come on, let's dance."

Shaking my head again, I emptied my energy drink. "I'm good."

"I bet you are," Chris said. "Now come on." He grabbed my hand and pulled me away from my safe space on the railing and dragged me down the stairs.

"No, please," I said, but my voice was just as weak as my attempt to resist his pull. When we reached the bottom of the stairs, I dropped my empty energy drink in a trash can as Chris kept dragging me through the crowd and onto the dance floor. And I danced. Somehow I danced. Feeling awkward at first, I needed a few moments to get into the rhythm of the music, but it got easier as I realized that no one around me gave a damn. I was just a guy on a dance floor moving to the music like everyone else. As I was beginning to feel one with the music and the crowd around me, I closed my eyes. Colored light still made it through my closed eyelids, throwing a dancing rainbow of soft, warm flashes on my retina. My heart was beating in sync with the rhythm of the beat booming in my ears, and I was sweating from every pore, beads of sweat running down my temples and my neck. For the first time in a long time, I felt like I was being myself, and no one was judging me.

I danced like that for I don't know how long, maybe ten minutes, maybe half an hour, and when I opened my eyes again, the crowd was still there but Chris was gone. From one moment to the next, I felt lost and insecure, as if he'd taken all my self-confidence and left me behind among strangers in a strange land. I continued dancing to keep myself from panicking, but unlike before, I felt like I had to concentrate to keep my limbs moving now. Always half a beat behind, I couldn't seem to get back in sync with the music, so I finally started moving toward the fringe of the dance floor where the lingerers started outnumbering the dancers, and then I just kept walking away. My sweat-soaked T-shirt clinging to my steaming torso, I was dying for something to drink but I was dying even more to take a leak, so I looked around until I spotted the LED-lit pictograms of a man and a woman above a glass swing door next to one of the bars.

The door led to a narrow, neon-lit aisle with one door on either end. Passing two kissing boys around my age, I headed for the men's room. When I entered, there was a guy of eighteen or nineteen standing at one of the urinals, but he was just finishing up his business, pulling up his zipper. As he passed me on my way to the urinal at the end of the room, he cast me an inviting smile, so I quickly averted my eyes. He was quite attractive, but on my first gay night out I was still too shy to strike up a conversation with a random stranger. Plus, I needed to go real bad.

Placing myself in front of the urinal, I unzipped and went about my business, closing my eyes and enjoying the cooling breeze coming from an open window. I was about halfway through dumping about a gallon when I heard soft moaning behind me. I turned my head. The moaning appeared to be coming from the occupied stall behind me, but it was not the kind of moan you do when you're taking a dump. There was also the sound of someone taking deep breaths through their nose, and I wasn't sure if both noises were coming from the same person. As I increased the pressure on my bladder to finish up my business, the moaning became louder and longer until it culminated in one final groan, followed by the rustling of clothes, the rattle of a belt buckle, and the sound of someone spitting into the toilet bowl. I moved my stream of urine to the center of the urinal to create an audible splash, and I cleared my throat for good measure, hoping that whoever was behind that door would have the decency to let me finish up and leave the restroom before they came out of their stall so we could avoid a potentially awkward situation. Naturally, I had no such luck.

I was still in the middle of letting things flow when the stall door behind me was unlocked and someone walked out. From the corner of my eye I saw a tall figure in dark clothes walk past the sinks. I turned my head to catch a glimpse of them as they pulled the door open and slipped outside. That's when a voice behind me made me jump.

"Oh, hey."

I looked over my shoulder to see Jack walking out of the same stall.

"Oh, uh," I said, averting my gaze and trying to finish up and tuck my junk away before my dick started sharing its opinion on what must have been going on in that stall in the last few minutes.

"Are you enjoying yourself?" Jack said, standing right next to me, leaning against the wall. If he had looked down, he'd have had a good luck at my private parts, which was kinda awkward, but he didn't. He looked straight at my face. I mean, as straight as you can look when your breath reeks of cheap vodka.

"Uh, no," I said, shaking my head. "Just taking a leak."

"No, I mean out there," he said, flicking his head at the door. "Where have you been keeping yourself? Haven't seen you since we got here."

I pulled up my zipper. "Yeah, no, I've been dancing. Quite a bit, actually."

"Cute. Come on, I need some fresh air."

Following him out of the room, I was heartened to see him stop at the sinks to wash his hands. It wasn't a small thing. You could be the awesomest person in the world, but if you didn't wash your hands after using the bathroom, I'd rather you didn't stand right next to me. And you could be a loud and obnoxious old potty mouth and still score a few points with me if you washed your hands after whatever sleazy things you chose to do in the bathroom. I was still washing mine as Jack wiped his wet hands dry on his pants, pulled the small vodka bottle out of his pocket, emptied it and dumped it in the trash can underneath the paper towel dispenser.

When I was done, he put his pleasantly cold hand on my neck and led me outside, down the corridor and toward a door at the end of the corridor. It led outside to an open-air terrace the size of a basketball court, scattered with kissing couples and small groups of three or four or five people engaged in animated conversations. I followed Jack across the terrace to a bench next to a big concrete butt bin. As he sat down, he pulled a crumpled pack of cigarettes out of his pants pocket and offered it to me. I shook my head and sat down next to him.

"No drinking, no smoking," Jack said, pulling a cigarette from the pack and putting it between his lips. He lit it and put the pack and lighter back in his pocket. "Do you have any vices at all?"

I tried hard to think of anything that would qualify as a vice and finally said, "I like pizza."

It made him laugh just when he was taking a drag on his cigarette, prompting a major coughing fit.

Patting his back, I said, "Have another cigarette, why don'tcha."

"Very funny," he croaked. As his coughing fit subsided, he spat on the floor and wiped his mouth. "Pizza is not a vice. Especially not for someone as skinny as you." He poked my ribs with his finger, making me flinch.

"Who knows, if I didn't binge on pizza I might be even skinnier."

"Right," he said, shaking his head. Then he touched my torso with the back of his hand. "Dude, you're soaking wet."

"I've been dancing."

He stuck his cigarette between his lips and took off his jacket. "Here, have my jacket."

"I'm good," I said, shaking my head.

"Bullshit. You're gonna catch pneumonia or something, and then you're gonna die, and then I'm gonna feel all guilty and depressed and shit, and then I'll have to drink more and take drugs to deal with it. You want me to drink more and take drugs?"

"No, but—"

"Well, there you go," he said, wrapping his jacket around my shoulders. "See, that didn't hurt, did it?"

"Thanks," I said, "But that's really not necessary."

"Dude!" Jack said, throwing his hands in the air. "Shut up already! I'm just trying to be nice, so what's your problem"?

He almost seemed hurt, and it made me feel bad. "Nothing. Sorry. I just didn't want to inconvenience you, that's all."

"Yeah, fuck that. Do I look inconvenienced? Listen, if you ever inconvenience me, I'll be sure to let you know in no uncertain terms, okay?"

"Okay," I said, nodding.

"Are you always like that?"

I frowned at him. "Like what?"

"Like, 'Oh, I'm so sorry, I didn't mean to inconvenience you,' and shit. What's up with that? If you're worried about being a burden on someone, you might as well go live in the desert and become a kermit or whatever."

"You mean a hermit?"

"Fuck you, smartass," he said, "Yes. Hermit. Kermit's that frog dude or something. Anyway, look, there are like, what, eight billion people in the world? Guess what, your existence is a burden on most of them. Not your family and friends and stuff. They'll be all like, 'Oh, little Uh-Timmy is such a nice little boy, and he always says please and thank you.' But to most everyone else, you're a major pain in the ass because you're eating their food and wasting their resources and shit, you know what I mean?"

"Uh," I said. "I'm not sure."

"Just think about it. We only have this one planet, and our resources are limited, right? And we're way too many people already. Every time you eat something, you're taking food away from someone who's starving. Now you can either blame yourself for things that are really beyond your control, or you can grow a spine and eat your pizza and then take a hot shower for half an hour without feeling guilty. And if you don't have a spine, become a politician and give nice little speeches about changing the world and then do absolutely nothing to actually do it. This is not complicated, so why the hell are we even talking about this?"

Stunned by Jack's rambling little speech, I didn't even know where to begin to pick apart his contradictions and inconsistencies, so I said, "Well, to be fair, you're doing most of the talking, so ... I don't know."

He glared at me for a moment, then he suddenly burst out laughing and brought his hand crushing down on my neck, rocking my body. "Dude! That's what I'm talking about! Don't be afraid to hurt my feelings, or anybody else's for that matter."

"Right."

"Anyway, my point is, just be yourself and stand up for it, you know? And whenever some random asshole comes along and offers you a random act of kindness, like lending you his jacket, just take it and say thank you and move on, okay?"

"Okay," I said. "Thank you."

"All right." He put his arm around me and leaned his head against my shoulder with a sigh. "I like you, you know?"

It was slightly awkward, but he didn't make any further moves, no attempts to kiss me or touch me inappropriately, so I just said, "Why, thank you, I like you too." We sat there in silence for a while until he pulled his phone out of his pocket, opened the camera app and stretched out his arm to take a selfie of us.

"Smile," he said, and I smiled, briefly resting my head against his as he took the photo.

We looked at it together, and it was a really good shot, even if my hair was a sweaty mess and Jack's sad eyes belied the smile on his lips.

As he put his phone away, my own phone chimed. I pulled it out of my pocket and unlocked the screen to find a text from you.

2-1 against Creekside! Guess who scored the winning goal?

With a smile, I typed my reply.

I bet you did. Congrats! You da man!

"Oh God, seriously?" Jack said. His head still resting against my shoulder, he'd been looking at the screen.

"What?" I said.

"'You da man?' What's with the brown-nosing?"

Hitting send, I said, "It's the kind of stuff he likes to hear. Sometimes he's needy like that." I shrugged, and Jack finally lifted his head off my shoulder and removed his arm.

"Yeah, no offense, but I think we both know who's the needy one here."

I looked at him. "You think I'm needy?"

"You think you're not?" Jack said, rolling his eyes. "All I hear is Tom, Tom, Tom, but it's not really about him, is it? It's about you. It's about what he thinks of you. And you think if you flatter him and tell him what he wants to hear, he'll like you. He should like you for telling him things he doesn't want to hear. You know, the unflattering, inconvenient stuff."

"Yeah, well," I said, averting my gaze, "it's complicated."

"Bullshit. Brain surgery is complicated. Friendship is simple. You like someone or you don't. You trust someone or you don't. If you don't trust someone to like you, the real you I mean, then that's not friendship, it's … I don't know what the hell it's called, but I bet there's a word for it. It's probably Greek or something."

"You wouldn't understand," I said in a low voice. It was a petty, unconscionable statement, because deep down inside I had a feeling he understood the situation better than I did.

My phone chimed again, and it was another text from you. *Hell yeah! & So where you at right now?*

"Shit," I uttered under my breath. What was I gonna tell you? That I was hanging out with Inka? She probably would have provided me with an alibi if I'd asked her, but I didn't want to lie to you again. I didn't want to be honest with you either.

"Go on," Jack said, peeking over my shoulder. "Tell him you're at a fag party with your fag friends."

I scoffed. "Yeah, right."

"You want me to do it for you?" he said, reaching for my phone, but I swatted his hand away.

"Dude, stop it already!"

"Stop what?" He reached for my phone again, but I blocked him with my body. The thought that he might get a hold of my phone and send you a message in my name freaked me out and got me all defensive, and by defensive I mean I went into attack mode.

"Stop lecturing me on honesty if you can't even be honest with yourself!"

"Whoa," he said, "what is that supposed to mean?"

"Your bullshit story about not being gay when you're getting toilet blow jobs at a gay club. Like, who are you trying to fool?"

He glared at me, and I could tell I hit him where it hurt. "And who am I hurting with this?" he says. "No one, that's who. Not that it's any of your fucking business."

"You're right, it's not. But just FYI, you're hurting yourself, so why would I take advice from someone with zero self-respect?" I shook off his jacket and tossed it back at him. "Thanks for the jacket."

As I turned on my heel and walked away, I heard Jack say, "So, you can be honest if you want to. Good job, pretty boy!"

"Screw you!" I said over my shoulder and I kept heading for the door.

Twelve

Ding-ding-dong, the doorbell went, and my heart sank to the bottom of the deep blue sea that was my soul on this Saturday morning after my first gay night out—a night that had started so promising, only to end in disaster. On my way back inside I had run into Chris and Sam who were looking for us because the place was about to close. I told them where Jack was, and while Sam went to fetch him, Chris looked at me, saw how I avoided his gaze, and asked the inevitable question.

"You okay?"

"Yeah, sure," I said. I really wasn't, and I would have loved to tell him all about the altercation with Jack and the texts from you, but there was no way to cover it all before Sam came back with Jack, and I didn't want to have that conversation in front of them. Especially not in front of Jack, obviously, and I was praying he wouldn't bring it up himself on our way back home. He didn't.

The mood in the car was very different from what it had been on the way in. Chris and Sam tried to engage us in light-hearted banter, drawing only monosyllabic responses from the unenthusiastic crowd in the back seat, so they quickly gave up, exchanging telling glances with raised eyebrows.

"Everything okay back there?" Chris asked, to which Jack responded with another burp, and I just said, "Yeah," while I kept typing my reply to your text asking me what I'd been up to.

Nothing, just hanging out. Anyway, tired now, gotta catch some sleep. Run tomorrow?

It was vague enough not to qualify as a blatant lie, but too vague to not raise your suspicion. Your elliptical reply was as quick as it was telling.

OK.

That was all. Just '*OK*,' and I could tell that everything was not okay. You knew something was up, and by not prying, you made sure I knew you knew. I stared at your message for a long time, wondering if there was anything I could say to make that crushing feeling go away, the feeling that something unspoken stood between us like a wall that nobody wanted but someone had to pay for. From the corner of my eye I could see Jack stretching his neck to peek at the screen of my phone, and when I turned my head to look at him, he quickly looked away, uttering, "Jesus fucking Christ," under his breath, prompting Chris to cast me a curious look in the rear view mirror.

Sam dropped me off first, which was fine by me because it denied Chris the chance to interrogate me about what had happened. When I reached my front door, I looked back. The car was still standing there with Chris and Sam staring down Jack who, judging by his body language, wasn't having any of it.

"Hey, get in here for a sec," my dad said when I tried to sneak past the living room where my parents were watching TV. They were sitting on the couch together, looking at me expectantly when I walked in, my hands buried in my pockets.

"What?" I said

"How was it?" Mom asked.

"Good."

"Did you enjoy yourself?"

"Yeah."

"Yeah?"

"Yeah."

"You drink anything?" Mom asked.

"Yes," I said, and when I saw the shocked look on her face, I added, "Two energy drinks. I told you they don't serve alcohol."

"Come here."

I approached her, and when I was close enough, she extended her neck like freaking Inspector Gadget and told me to breathe.

"Mom!" I said, and that was already enough.

"Go brush your teeth," she said, crumpling her nose. "And don't stay on your phone all night."

I sighed. "Good night."

"Night, Tim."

"Night, buddy."

By the time I got out of the shower, I had two new text messages. When I saw the notification LED blinking, I was hoping they weren't from you. When they weren't, I was disappointed.

The first message was from Chris.

Please tell me Jack wasn't hitting on you.

I laid down on my bed and typed my reply.

Jack wasn't hitting on me.

The second message was from Inka.

How did it go? Sorry I couldn't be there!

Inka had wanted to come with us, but she had to attend her grandma's 69th-birthday dinner. I still felt awkward around her because of what had happened, but now I wondered how the evening would have gone if she'd been there to chaperon me. In spite of the awkwardness, I probably would have been clinging to her all evening, so that altercation with Jack probably never would have happened, and even if it had, she would have been able to arbitrate between us to prevent the worst. Either way, I didn't feel like going over all the spilled milk with her tonight, so I kept my reply short.

All right. Anyway, gotta hit the sack now. TTYL.

By the time I hit send, Chris had sent me another text.

Good! I still got that hedge trimmer, you know? ;)

I appreciated his attempt at lighthearted fun, but I didn't want to discuss what had happened with him either, so I put my phone away and went to sleep. Not that I got any, at least not until the early morning hours, and now I felt like a zombie, and the last thing I wanted to do was jog around the neighborhood with you.

"Tim!" I heard Dad call from downstairs. "Tom is here!"

"In a minute!" I shouted back. With my heart nervously pounding in my chest, I swung my heavy legs out of bed, put on my running gear in slow motion, and schlepped myself down the stairs.

You were sitting at the counter with my dad, holding a glass of orange juice and peeking at the screen of Dad's laptop. He usually hated when people watched him writing, but he was too polite to say anything.

"Wow," you said when you saw me shuffling into the kitchen. "You look like shit."

Dad clearly didn't appreciate your diction, but by the way he peered at me over the rim of his glasses I could tell he shared your sentiment.

"Everything okay, buddy?"

"Just tired," I said with a croaky voice, opening the fridge. When I lifted the orange juice carton, I could tell by its weight there was about half a swig left in it. Closing the fridge door, I glared at you. "Really?"

With an impish grin, you offered me your glass. "Have mine."

I took the glass and shoved the empty carton in your hand. You got up and took it to the trash, but I could see the surprise eating into your grin. You were not used to being told to clean up after yourself, especially not by me, but I was on the verge of snapping. I'd had a lot of time for introspection last night, and what I had found was a dark anger brewing inside of me. I was angry at me, my situation, my life, and pretty much everyone who was playing a supporting role in this farce. And sorry, not sorry, but that included you. I was scared to tell you the truth, and that was first and foremost my own problem, but there had to be a reason why I was more scared of your reaction than that of others, so my problem wouldn't have been as much of a problem if it hadn't been for you.

I emptied the glass and took it to the sink for rinsing. "Where's Mom?"

"Hardware store," Dad said. "She's getting a new blade for the lawn mower."

"I love the unconventional gender roles in your family, Mr. Fogel," you said, your eyes trained on me.

Dad looked at you. "Do you now?"

"Absolutely. You know, like, how Mrs. Fogel is wearing the pants around here while you ..." Your voice trailed off.

"Go on," Dad said.

You shook your head. "No, I mean, I'm just saying. Your wife is spending her Saturday morning at the hardware store while you're sitting here being … you know, all artsy-fartsy. Where I come from, that's kind of unusual."

Dad looked at his computer screen. "You need to get out more and expand your horizon, Tom. You can start by getting out of my kitchen so I can continue being *artsy-fartsy*."

I kicked the heel of your shoe. "Are we gonna stand here all day or are we gonna run? Come on."

"What about breakfast?" Dad asked.

"After my run," I said, and he shrugged.

"Nice day, Mr. Fogel," you said and walked toward the front door. I followed you, casting a glance back at my dad. He winked at me, but there was a sadness in his eyes that gave my heart a sting. He knew what I was going through with you, and it hurt him, but there was nothing he could do about it. There was nothing anyone could do about it, except me.

We ran our regular route, and we did it in silence as always, but something was different today. Where we usually ran side by side, you now made sure to run two steps ahead of me and never let me catch up. Whenever I increased my speed, you did the same or you swerved into the middle of the sidewalk to block my way. You played this stupid game for two blocks until I finally gave up and stayed behind you, because if we'd have kept going at this speed, we would have been drained in no time. You still maintained a higher-than-usual pace, and I suppose you did it because you didn't trust me not to put myself in front of you with a surprise burst. What had I ever done to make you think I could be petty like that?

As we passed the soccer field in the park, you suddenly raised your hand, slowed down and eventually stopped. Stooping over and propping your hands against your knees, you were panting like a dog as you said, "Take a break?"

"Sure," I said.

You walked over to the next bench and sat down. It was the exact same bench I'd been sitting down with Chris the other day, because sometimes life was funny like that. Except in my life sometimes meant most of the time, and it was really not funny at all. I sat next to you as you reclined and put your elbows on the backrest of the bench, taking deep breaths through clenched teeth.

"You all right?" I said.

You shook your head. "Side stitch. Probably went too fast."

"You think?" I said, not even bothering to conceal the snark in my voice, but you didn't take the bait. We sat there in silence for a minute or two, looking at the soccer game that was going on.

"You should play soccer again," you finally said when some cute redhead scored a goal.

"Nah, I'm good," I say. "Not enjoying team sports as much as I used to."

You scoffed. "You're such a loner."

"Maybe. But I like it that way." After a pause, I added, "You used to like me that way, too."

"What are you talking about?" You playfully slapped the back of my head. "I still like you, you dweeb."

I looked at you. "Oh yeah?"

"Yeah," you said, resting your hand on my shoulder. Its softness and warmth matched your voice, and I felt myself soften too as my body soaked up your warmth like a sponge. Nearly overwhelmed by my feelings for you, the temptation to finally tell you the truth had never been so strong. I took a deep breath, and then I heard myself say, "Wanna hang out later?"

How stupid was that? I wanted to kick myself, that's how stupid it was. Crushed by my continuing inability to do the right thing at the right time, I suddenly felt the urge to get up and run away as fast as I could and never see you or anyone else I knew ever again.

You withdrew your hand from my shoulder and said, "Oh, uh, sorry, but I already have plans with Maia."

"Oh."

"Yeah. My parents are out all day, so … you know." You made a lewd hand gesture, which was completely unnecessary. It didn't take a genius to guess what you guys would be up to, and I clearly wasn't a genius. I was just a stupid, cowardly little fag who couldn't even bring himself to tell his best friend he's gay.

"Right, okay. Never mind then."

"Maybe you can do something with Inka?"

"Yeah, maybe," I said, standing up. "Anyway, come on. I don't want to sit here all day."

I started running, and you followed me, staying two steps behind me all the way home.

Thirteen

"Why, hello there, pretty boy," Milo said, interrupting his table-wiping to look at me, tilting his head and putting one hand to his hip as I walked into the Korova. His enthusiastic smile quickly went to hide in a tree when he saw me waving my hand dismissively as I walked past him with a grunt. He followed me to my booth. "Oh, wow, somebody didn't get laid last night."

I slid into the booth, put my left elbow on the table and propped the side of my face against my hand with a sigh. Yes, I was putting on a show. I usually didn't wear my heart on my sleeve like that, but today I let it be known to my audience of one that I was in a bad place and needed help. Milo was the only person I knew who was more than twice my age, *and* he was gay, so maybe he actually knew what he was talking about unlike everyone else I knew.

"So what will it be?" he said. He was still smiling, but it was no longer that phony, over the top I-love-all-my-paying-customers smile. This one was genuine, warm and sympathetic, but at the same time unobtrusive. It seemed to say, 'I'm here if you need me, but no pressure.' Or maybe that's just what I wanted it to say because it's what I needed to hear.

"Scotch," I said. "On the rocks."

"Yeah," he said softly, "I can tell a scotch is exactly what you need right now, honey, but how about I bring you an extra strong Double Dark Chocolate milkshake? With extra chocolate."

I exhaled. "Go on then."

"Coming right up."

Two minutes later he was back with two extra strong Double Dark Chocolate milkshakes, placing them between us as he slid into the bench opposite me. I turned my head to look around. There were only three other guests.

"How's business?" I said, pulling my milkshake toward me.

He shrugged and shook his head. "Can't complain. Early Saturday afternoons are always slow, but ask me again in three hours and I won't have time to answer because the place will be buzzing."

The straw in my mouth, I nodded, sucking in the thick, cold, bitter-sweet liquid. He did the same, his piercing eyes trained on me, waiting for me to start the conversation we both knew we were about to have. I swallowed, wiped my lips with the back of my hand and said, "Have you ever been in love with someone you knew you couldn't have?"

He threw his head back and laughed. "Who hasn't, honey?"

My face flushed. Apparently I had asked a particularly stupid question.

"Is that's what's going on?" Milo asked.

"It's part of the problem."

"I see."

"Yeah. So, what's the best way to deal with it?"

Milo looked at me for a long moment before he said, "There is none. There's no best way to deal with anything, frankly. There may be good ways and not so good ways, but it depends on so many moving parts. When it comes to any kind of tricky situations, my mother always says, 'Whichever way you do it is probably wrong.'"

I snorted. "Great."

"Do they know? I mean, the person you're in love with. Do they know you're in love with them?"

"Hell no."

"So how do you know you can't have them?"

"I'm gay," I said, looking Milo straight in the eyes. "He's not."

Milo sighed. "Oh boy."

"I know. Also, he's my best friend, so he must never know I'm in love with him, because that would destroy everything."

"Maybe," Milo said. "But he does know you're gay, right?"

I shook my head. "But I'm gonna tell him. I mean, I want to tell him, I just haven't found the right moment yet."

"Just don't wait too long. This is not going to get any easier, you know? If he's your best friend and you drag your feet with this, he'll ask the legitimate question what took you so long."

"I'll do it," I said. "Soon."

"Good." He took a swig of his milkshake. "Now let me tell you a story that happened to me a long, long time ago. First week of my sophomore year, high school, not college, I noticed this new kid in school, a freshman, and I immediately fell for him. He was incredibly cute with his curly blond hair and his green eyes and that dazzling smile and everything, and I wanted him. I wanted to be his friend, and I wanted him to be my lover, so I started teasing him whenever I saw him in school or on our way to school, and bless him, he liked being teased. Teasing became banter, and our banter eventually turned into this very fragile friendship. It wasn't a very close friendship, but we did hang out every once in a while. It was complicated. He was doing sports, I was doing art, so there wasn't all that much we had in common, although we did share the same sense of humor and the same taste in music. Anyway, that was twenty years ago, and things were still very different for gay people. I mean, they were already better than thirty or forty years ago, but they were still not easy, especially if you were shy like me."

"Shy?" I chuckled. "You?"

"Believe it or not, yes. This beautiful butterfly was still a fat, ugly caterpillar. So anyway, we hung out together, and I desperately wanted to have more happen between us, but I was so shy, and I could never figure out if it was safe to make a pass at him, because I had no idea if he was gay or not. There were times when he made allusions about gay sex and he almost seemed to challenge me to make a move, but there were other times when he was that extremely masculine jock type of person, and I thought there's no way he's gay. To be honest, whenever the gay sex topic came up, I thought he was setting up a trap and waiting for me to walk right into it so he could tell me to back the fuck off and then go walk around and tell people he got hit on by a fucking faggot."

"Right," I said, and I couldn't help but think of you and what you would do if I ever made a pass at you. "So, what happened?"

"I took my chance, eventually, years after we'd first met. My senior year was about to come to an end and I was going to be off to college in a different city soon, and there was a good chance I'd never see him again, so on my last regular day of school, I walked up to him and told him I wanted to fuck him."

I laughed. "Just like that?"

"Yeah, well, I think I didn't say 'fuck'. I told him my parents were out of town and I wanted to have sex with him, so I told him to come over to my place that evening."

"And he did?"

"He did indeed."

"Wow."

"I know! But don't you get the wrong idea now. I'm not telling you this story so you can run off and do something completely crazy or reckless or something like that. My point is, I probably could have had sex with him a whole lot sooner. Like, years sooner, if I'd only had the guts to just go for it. And then my whole life might have gone down a completely different path. So, what I'm trying to tell you is, if you want to do something, do it. Don't wait for some magical right moment, because chances are that moment will never come, or even worse, when it comes you might not even recognize it. There is no perfect moment, whatever happens, happens, and according to my mother, everything, even something bad, is good for something, but there's only one way to find out."

"Your mother is a very wise woman."

"Thanks," Milo said. "I'd tell her you said that, but she's already too full of herself. But just so you know, I never went wrong taking her advice."

I exhaled audibly. "All right. I'll do it. Whatever 'it' means. But yeah. I'm gonna do something."

"Good," Milo said. "Just be yourself and do what you think is right, and always keep in mind, you're not alone. You got friends, and if all else fails, you can always come here for more wise words from my mother."

"Okay. Thanks."

"You're welcome, sweetheart." He cast a glance over my shoulder. "Anyway, I think your date is here."

"My what?" I turned my head, and there was this guy standing behind me. His hands buried in his pockets, he was keeping a safe ten-foot distance and smiling a shy, awkward smile. He was tall and skinny, with short dark hair, and I thought I recognized him from school, although I had never talked to him. He may have been a junior, but I wasn't sure.

"Come on," Milo said to him. "Don't be shy."

"I ... I'm sorry," he said in a low, shaky voice. "I didn't mean to interrupt."

Milo shook his head and picked up his glass. "Oh, no no, you're not interrupting anything. I got a business to run anyway." He cast me a parting glance, winked, and disappeared behind the counter.

Meanwhile, the skinny guy approached me, clearing his throat. "Uh, hi. Sorry, I ..." He laughed. "This is awkward. I'm Aidan. I think we're going to the same school? Brookhurst High?"

I nodded slowly, holding on to my milkshake with both hands to keep them from trembling because I had no idea what was happening. "I think I've seen you around. I'm Tim."

"Right," he said, pulling his hand out of his pocket and scratching the back of his head. "I was just wondering ... did I see you at the Unicorn Club last Friday?"

My heart was pounding in my chest like a jackhammer, and my ears felt like they were about to burst into flames. "Oh, uh, I ... I'm not ... I think ... maybe?"

"You probably haven't seen me, though, because you were dancing with your eyes closed."

"Oh," I said, averting my gaze and trying hard to conceal a smile. "Yeah."

Into the ensuing awkward pause, Aidan made an indistinct gesture toward the bench opposite me and said, "Okay if I sit?"

"Oh! Sorry, yeah. Sure. I mean … yeah."

By the time he slid into the bench, Milo was back. "What can I get you, darling?"

"Diet Coke, please?"

"Sure." Milo looked at me. "Anything else for you?"

I'd nearly finished my milkshake. An empty glass would have given me an easy way out, an excuse to get up and leave if I felt too overwhelmed with this unexpected situation, but with my heart rate finally decreasing to reasonable levels, I was beginning to feel intrigued with the strange figure sitting across the table. Nodding at Milo, I said, "I'll have another one."

"Good," Milo said as if this was the only acceptable answer, and he left us alone again.

"So," Aidan said.

"So."

"Sorry to barge in on you like this, but I've just seen you, passing by … I mean, I was passing by, not you, obviously, and I thought maybe …" His voice trailed off.

"Maybe?"

He chuckled nervously. "I'm sorry. I'm not very good at this. I don't usually do this kind of thing. You know, approaching random strangers to strike up a conversation. Except you're not a stranger. I mean, not really, because I've seen you around at school. And at the club the other day."

"Right," I said. "So, I'm not a stranger, just random?"

This time we both chuckled, and I was beginning to feel more relaxed because apparently I was talking to someone who was a whole lot more nervous than I was. I'd never thought that would ever be a thing, but here we were.

"I didn't see your friend, though," Aidan said.

I wasn't quite sure who he was referring to. "My friend?"

"You know, the guy you always hang out with at school?"

139

"Oh, Tom," I said, shaking my head. "No, no, he's not … we're not … I mean, he's my best friend, but he's not … into that whole gay thing."

"Right."

"It's complicated."

"I see," he said. "Well, anyway, I've seen you at the club and I recognized you from school, so when I came passing by just now and I saw you in here, I thought I'd ask you, if you'd maybe like to, uh—"

Milo arrived and placed our orders on the table. "Enjoy," he whispered as if not to interrupt, winking at me again before he scurried away.

"—grab a Coke and a milkshake sometime?" I finished Aidan's sentence for him.

He grinned awkwardly. "Yeah."

"Well," I said and started sucking on my milkshake.

Scratching his head, Aidan said, "I guess I have to come up with something else now, huh?"

"You could try."

He paused to think for a second, taking a swig of Coke before he said, "Do you like pizza?"

He wasn't taking a great risk with this question, but that was fine by me. "I *love* pizza."

"No way!" he said, his eyes wide open in mock surprise. "I love pizza too. Like, what are the odds, right?"

"Infinitesimal." I had no idea who was operating my vocal apparatus on my behalf, but it couldn't have been me, because when I talked to strangers I usually was a nervous mess and not in the mood for banter. I didn't know why today was any different, but it was.

"So, uh, how would you like to, you know, grab some pizza sometime? I'm thinking Friday night, maybe?"

My heart sank because I had promised you to be at the game Friday night. "I would love to," I said, "but I'm afraid I can't. I already have plans on Friday."

"Oh," he said, trying hard to maintain his smile, but his disappointment was palpable.

"It's Tom. He's playing soccer on Fridays. I missed his last game, so I promised him I'd be there for the next one."

He nodded. "Never mind then. Maybe some other time."

"Yeah," I said, feeling miserable for having broken his spirit. He didn't even try to offer Thursday or Wednesday or any other alternative day. "Unless …"

He looked at me.

"You don't happen to like soccer, do you?"

A smile flashed across his face. "I love soccer, actually. Well, soccer players, mostly, but yeah."

"No way," I said in mock surprise like he had before. "I love soccer too. What are the odds?"

"Infinitesimal?"

"Probably. So maybe, if you like, we can watch the game together and grab some pizza afterward?"

"I'd love to," he said, beaming like the sun.

"It's a date then, I guess." As I grabbed my glass, my glance fell on Milo. Standing behind the counter and polishing a glass, he was ostentatiously avoiding my gaze with a wide grin on his face.

FOURTEEN

High up in the bleachers of Brookhurst High, Aidan was sitting close to me. Very close. The way I liked to sit with you on my bed when we were playing video games and our arms or legs inadvertently touched more often than not. I cherished these moments because it was the only form of physical contact between us that was innocent and devoid of any meaning beyond my clandestine satisfaction of feeling closer to you than I ever would have been allowed to be. I wondered if that was what Aidan was doing here, sitting close to me and pretending it didn't mean anything when our legs touched.

I'm not going to deny it, I'd been feeling nervous about tonight, about being seen with Aidan in public. After our first official meeting at the Korova, I had parsed my memory to find potential recollections or randomly saved images of previous encounters, and much to my surprise, I had found some. There had been that one time we bumped into each other in the hallway between classes, and he apologized with a shy smile. At the time I thought it was off, because usually whenever someone accidentally bumped into me at school, especially someone older, I'd get the stink eye and be told to watch where I was going. I didn't think much of it at the time, because I was too busy walking and talking with you, but in hindsight, Aidan's unexpected politeness spoke to his character and maybe even to something more than that. Remembering Aidan's shy smile that day triggered more memories of fleeting moments that had never even registered with me at the time. I remembered sitting in the school cafeteria during lunch a few months back, having an animated discussion with you about *The Last Jedi* and whether or not anyone should care about who Rey's parents were, when my eyes randomly grazed the cafeteria and caught Aidan looking at me from across the room. When our eyes met, he quickly looked away, and that was that. Again, I didn't think much of it, because that kind of thing happened all the time. Two random strangers' eyes randomly met, and then one of them or both looked away, and it didn't mean anything. At least most of the time it didn't. But then I remembered that other time our eyes met. It was Pride Day last year, and Aidan was wearing a rainbow-colored *Pride* T-shirt to school. This time it was me who was staring at him from across the schoolyard as he was surrounded by his friends, and when our eyes met, it was me who quickly looked away, but not too quickly to notice the shy smile on his lips when he saw me. I'm not going to say me looking at him that day didn't mean anything, because it did. It meant I was intrigued, and I was secretly hoping that one day I'd be wearing a *Pride* T-shirt to school and all my friends, including you, would be standing around me and it wouldn't be a big deal for anyone. Not for me, not for you, not for anyone. I'd just be out and proud, and in the distance, a blessing of unicorns would be peeing rainbows across the sky. Did you know a group of unicorns is called a blessing?

Nothing means nothing.

Everything means something.

The reason I had been feeling nervous about tonight was because I was basically having a date in public with someone who was openly gay. As much as I wished it weren't, this was a big thing for me. It was a big first step on a journey I'd been putting off for way too long, and I was proud to finally having found the courage to take that step. First steps were always scary. Unlike you, I'd never been one to throw myself headfirst into the unknown, reveling in the spine-tingling excitement that came with it and craving that adrenaline rush. Between you and me, I had always been the timid one. Remember that one time your parents took us to Six Flags Magic Mountain, and I didn't want to get on the Full Throttle roller coaster? You kept encouraging me, badgering me, goading me until I finally gave in, and after the ninety most thrilling seconds of my life, I wanted to go again, and again, and again until you eventually got annoyed with me and wanted to move on. But before you got annoyed with me and my newly discovered love for thrill rides, I could see the proud look in your eyes. Sitting in the bleachers with Aidan was almost as thrilling as going on the Full Throttle for the first time, but I somehow doubted you'd feel the same sense of pride about it you felt back at Six Flags. It made me wonder if back then, you hadn't actually been proud of me for having overcome my fear. Maybe you had simply been proud of yourself for having pushed me to do it.

When we took our seats in the bleachers, the teams were already done with the warm up and had made their way back into the locker rooms for their final pre-game preparations, so you were still unaware of me and Aidan. While we were waiting for the game between our Brookhurst Bobcats against Fullerton FC to begin, we watched the bleachers fill up. A lot of looks came flying our way, some of them bemused, some apparently charmed. Not to generalize, but most of my peers' looks seemed to belong in the former category, most of Aidan's in the latter. Some of his friends waved at him, and he waved back. None of the people I knew waved at me.

As the teams entered the pitch, the Bobcats battle song started blasting from the loudspeakers, and everyone in the bleachers was on their feet clapping, cheering, chanting. It was a well-rehearsed choreography, familiar to everyone who attended Bobcats games on a regular basis—like me, and, as it turned out, like Aidan. I had never noticed him at games before, but he was on his feet even faster than me. He knew the chants, he knew the tunes, and all of a sudden we had one more thing in common that I hadn't expected.

I sought you out as you took your position at the center line right before kick-off, and when our eyes finally met, I waved at you with both arms like an aircraft marshaller telling an airplane to stop before it crashes into the terminal. You waved back at me with a heartening smile, but when you saw who I was standing next to, your smile snap-froze into a grimace as if someone had doused you in liquid nitrogen.

"Go, Tom!" Aidan shouted out next to me, and while I wished he wouldn't do that, I felt compelled to do the same. "Go, go, Tom!"

"God, those legs," Aidan said with a sigh.

"Whose legs?" I asked, wondering if he was swooning over you and how I would feel about it if he did.

"All of them, really."

I chuckled, sort of relieved. "Right."

"It's a shame none of these guys are gay. At least none we're aware of."

"Tell me about it," I uttered under my breath, but he must have heard me. From the corner of my eye I saw him scrutinize my face, perhaps waiting for me to elaborate, but he didn't say anything, and I didn't offer anything further.

We took our seats, at least for a few moments. The game was off to a furious start with Fullerton attacking from the kick off and hitting the goal post after less than a minute. The audience were back on their feet and saw you clap your hands and bark at your stunned team mates, telling them to wake up and take control. What followed was a series of fast-paced attacks and counter-attacks that kept the audience on their toes, chanting and clapping throughout the entire first half of the game.

"Damn, he's good," Aidan said somewhere halfway through, and he was right. You were playing one of the best games I could remember, incessantly pushing your team mates forward, directing attack after attack.

"Yeah," I said, proud to be your friend.

Some forty minutes into the game, you entered the penalty box from the right, holding the ball close to your foot. You started to dribble, and the Fullerton defender stepped on your foot with no chance to get to the ball. You took the fall, and without hesitation, the referee blew his whistle and pointed to the penalty spot. As the crowd in the bleachers went crazy, your team mates huddled around you to pat your back and ruffle your hair, but you were not having any of it. You wrestled yourself free and grabbed the ball. You had once told me it was considered bad luck for the player who got fouled to shoot the penalty himself. You had also told me it was a stupid superstition, so I wasn't surprised to see you place the ball on the penalty spot and wait for everyone else to clear the penalty box.

Another whistle, and after four powerful strides you hammered the ball in the top right corner of the goal, leaving the goalkeeper no chance. To a deafening roar from the crowd I jumped up and down with my arms in the air. As the Bobcats battle song started blasting from the loudspeakers, I noticed Aidan moving next to me, and when I turned my head, I saw him doing the floss dance to the beat of the music.

Do you even know how much I loved the floss dance?

I had loved it ever since it had gone viral after that Backpack Kid did it during Katy Perry's performance on SNL. Heck, I had even practiced in front of a mirror myself, not that I had ever planned on doing it in public. But now, in desperate need to utilize the rush of endorphins your magnificent penalty goal had released into my veins, I joined Aidan in doing the floss dance before I even knew it. I looked at him, he looked back at me, and we both laughed and kept flossing to the beat of the music. When I turned my head back to the field to find you, you were emerging from the huddle of your team mates who had all come to congratulate you on your goal. Just as I turned toward the field, you turned toward the bleachers to accept your well-deserved cheers, your arms raised high, the smile on your face outshining the floodlights. Still flossing, I had my eyes trained on you, waiting for your gaze to find me. When it finally did and you saw me and Aidan celebrating your success, your smile quickly disappeared and it kidnapped my own smile and took it somewhere where they both died together. Thrown off my rhythm, I was grateful the music stopped blasting from the loudspeakers, giving me an excuse to stop dancing and sitting back down.

"That was awesome!" Aidan said, sitting back down next to me.

"Yeah," I said, trying hard to maintain my enthusiasm.

"You okay?"

"Sure," I said, but Aidan wasn't fooled. He looked at me for a while, waiting for me to meet his gaze, but when I kept pretending not to notice, he said, "He has no idea, has he?"

I shook my head.

"Oh well," Aidan said, nudging me with his elbow. "He's your friend. He'll understand."

I was beginning to wonder what fueled everyone's optimism about your tolerance and your capacity to understand. Maybe they saw something I didn't because I was too close to you. Maybe I could only see the details from up close, and only a handful of them at a time but never the big picture that someone would see when they looked at you from a distance.

The game continued. After your goal, the Bobcats were the dominating team now, running attack after attack. The team was oozing confidence from every pore of their skin, and a second goal seemed only a matter of time. But seconds before halftime, a Fullerton player intercepted a pass near the center line, broke through the Bobcats' last line of defense, and upon seeing the Bobcats' goalkeeper standing too far in front of his goal, he lobbed the ball over the goalkeeper's head and into the net. It was a great goal, only for the wrong team, and it noticeably dampened the mood as the teams made the way to the locker rooms at halftime.

The second half was almost the exact opposite of the first. Fullerton launched attack after attack, and the Bobcats rarely made it out of their own half. It was almost as if they had left all their confidence back in the locker room, but at least their defense was holding up, not allowing Fullerton to score for more than half an hour.

With ten minutes left to go, after another thwarted Fullerton chance, the crowd started chanting as if on cue, realizing the team needed their support. We were not content with a tie. We wanted the team to win, and we wanted the team to know they could. Whoever was in charge of the music picked up on the mood that was trying to spill from the bleachers onto the field, and they played the Bobcats battle song again. People rose to their feet, cheering, chanting, dancing, and Aidan and I started flossing again. We were all trying to transfer our energy to the team, and the team noticed. They saw what was going on in the bleachers, and they knew they owed it to us, and to themselves, to give their last everything. And indeed, the Bobcats were finally on the offense again, running a series of fierce attacks on Fullerton's goal. Two minutes left. A corner kick came flying into the penalty box. The goalkeeper got his fingers on the ball but he couldn't hold on to it. A Fullerton defender tried to kick the ball away, but his kick was blocked by two Bobcats. There was a huge commotion as a dozen players from both sides were trying to get control of the ball. For a moment, no one seemed to know what was going on until all of a sudden, the ball somehow scrambled across the line.

I couldn't explain what happened next, even if I tried. I turned to Aidan, and Aidan turned to me, and we were both jumping up and down, cheering, our arms up in the air, and I don't know who made the first move. Maybe it was him, maybe it was me, or maybe it was neither of us and what happened just happened naturally, but before I even knew it, we both wrapped our arms around each other, still jumping up and down. It was the weirdest feeling in the world. The closest I had ever come to hugging another boy like that was when I used to wrestle with you when we were younger, or when you put me in a headlock to give me a noogie. This was different from how Chris had hugged me good-bye after we'd first met. That one had been a soft, gentle, tender hug. This one was boisterous, powerful, and raw, and I liked it. I loved it, because it lacked the latent violence, the sense of coercion that came with wrestling you. This was the pure, unbridled joy I would forever be denied when I was with you.

I don't know how long it lasted, probably too long not to mean anything, but just like neither of us had started it, neither of us needed to be told when it was time to let go. It just happened naturally, and when our eyes met after our hug, there was no feeling of unease or awkwardness. I held Aidan's gaze for a little longer than necessary, and it was that extra second or two that made all the difference. Two guys hugging when their favorite team scored a goal didn't mean anything per se, but one brief look could change everything forever.

As I turned back to the field to seek you out, Aidan kept his hand on my shoulder for a little while, squeezing it ever so gently. I cast a brief smile back at him, putting my hand on his and squeezing it back. Meanwhile, you emerged from the celebratory huddle of Bobcats, and from the demeanor of yourself and everyone around you, it seemed you had played a substantial part in scoring this goal. I tried to catch your eye, but in this moment of triumph, you were too busy waving to the crowd and receiving their acclamation.

There were two minutes of play left, but the Bobcats lined up around the penalty box and built an impenetrable wall to defend their lead against Fullerton's last-ditch efforts to score. When the final whistle blew, a relieved cheer from the crowd sounded through the lush evening air. Aidan high-fived me and shouted, "Yeah, Bobcats!"

Tugging his sleeve, I said, "Come on."

"Where are we going?"

"Guard of honor!"

I grabbed his hand and started pulling him away, along our row of seats and toward the stairs. It was just a few steps, but they were the first steps I had ever walked holding hands with a guy. His hand was bigger than mine, but it was soft and warm, and while the thought of it was thrilling and emboldening, I didn't feel quite comfortable enough yet to hold on to Aidan's hand all the way down the stairs, passing dozens of people along the way. So I let go of him as we made our way down, but I turned my head every few steps to make sure he was still behind me. When we reached the field, we stood for a guard of honor with dozens of other elated Bobcats fans, high-fiving the players as they made their way back into the locker room. You were the last one to make your way inside, your arms spread wide to high five people on either side. Aidan and I were standing to your right, our hands in the air to high five you, but just before you reached us, you withdrew your right hand to wipe sweat from your face. You might as well have flipped me the bird right to my face. It was a disparaging, contemptuous gesture, but it was also surprisingly weak and almost cowardly, because you didn't even have the guts to look me in the eyes. And to think that for the past few months I had been tormenting myself, feeling like a coward for not being able to reveal my true feelings to you. As soon as you had passed us, you extended your hand again to high five the last few people before you disappeared in the tunnel to the locker rooms.

"No offense, but that was kinda cheap," Aidan said as the guard of honor dissipated around us.

I just shrugged, because I was afraid if I said anything, my voice might crack.

Aidan put his hand on my shoulder. "I'm sorry. Maybe I shouldn't have come."

"Don't you dare," I said, glaring at him. I sounded angrier than I intended, so I pinched the bridge of my nose and tried to take the edge out of my voice. "Don't you dare let his ass-hole behavior make you feel bad. I've been doing that for way too long."

"Right," he said in a low voice. "I'm just saying."

I exhaled, burying my hands in my pockets. We stood there for a few moments, unsure what to say or do. Swallowing the lump in my throat, I fought back tears of anger.

"Look," Aidan finally said, "I understand if you don't feel like getting pizza anymore. Maybe we should just call it a night? Take a rain check?"

As I looked at him, at his warm eyes and the restrained smile on his lips, I realized how I wasn't used to being told it was okay to feel the way I felt. All I'd ever known was people rolling their eyes at me, telling me to man up or get a grip and not be such a wuss, and I was so sick and tired of it all.

"Now you listen to me," I said in a low but adamant voice, poking Aidan's chest with my finger as my anger slowly turned into resolve. "If this thing between us is going to work, here's what you need to understand about me: I will never *ever* not feel like getting pizza, you hear me?"

"Yes, sir," he said in mock reverence, feigning an intimidated little puppy look.

"I'm glad I've made myself clear," I said with a stern look on my face. Then I grabbed his hand and started dragging him toward the exit.

Fifteen

Ding-dong, the doorbell went, and it was the most devastating sound I ever could have imagined on a Saturday morning at ten. It was as humiliating as a slap in the face, as painful as a punch in the gut, and as terrifying as a drooling, barking pit bull let off his leash. If you were ready to relinquish your signature doorbell ring tone, what else were you ready to give up on? Then again, you were still here, so maybe all was not lost. Not yet anyway.

Mom and Dad exchanged an anxious look as I dropped the spoon in my cereal bowl and got off my chair. I hadn't told them anything yet, but they knew us well enough to know something was up. They had known for a few days now, but they'd been kind enough not to ask me about it. Nevertheless, I did feel their gazes sticking to the back of my neck as I made my way to the front door and pulled it open.

When I saw it was really you and not the mailman, my heart started beating a little faster, and I breathed a silent sigh of relief. "Hey," I said with a smile that felt genuinely insecure.

"Hey," you said with no smile on your lips, your eyes lifeless and cold.

"Want to come in?"

You shook your head. "Actually, can we get going? I'm meeting Maia later."

"Oh, okay."

"Morning, Tom," my parents sounded in unison from the kitchen.

"Yeah, hi," you said with a lackadaisical wave of your hand.

"I'm off," I said over my shoulder as I stepped outside.

"Have fun," Dad said, and I wondered if he was trolling me.

As you turned around and started jogging toward the sidewalk, I pulled the door shut and followed you. This time, you made no effort to stay two steps ahead of me. You had me running right by your side, as if you were offering me the chance to strike up a conversation, but I was saving my breath for now. Once again we made it halfway through the park until you stopped and sat on one of the benches lining the soccer field where a bunch of grown ups were playing today.

"Side stitches again?" I said as I sat down next to you.

"No," you said, interlocking your fingers on the top of your head and looking across the soccer field. "Just want to take a break."

We sat in silence for a few moments, and I knew I could no longer ignore the big, fat elephant that was sitting right between us. "Great game yesterday," I eased you into the topic.

"Did you enjoy yourself?" you said without looking at me, the snark in your voice cutting like a rusty knife.

"Of course."

Finally, you turned your head and looked at me. "So, you enjoy hanging out with fags now?"

My first impulse was to pretend I had no idea what you were even talking about, but your use of the word 'fag' infuriated me more than it ever had before.

"Don't say that," I said, avoiding your gaze.

"Say what?"

I glared at you, my face flushing. "Don't call people fags."

"Or what?" you challenged me, holding my glare.

"Nothing. Just don't. It's a horrible word, and using it makes you sound like a horrible person."

You snorted. "At least I'm not a fag."

"Jesus Christ, stop it!" I said, raising my voice. "What is wrong with you?"

"With me? What is wrong with *you*, Tim? Standing in the bleachers and shaking your ass like a goddamn homo, it's a fucking embarrassment! What the hell were you thinking?"

"Nothing. For once, I wasn't thinking anything and just enjoying myself. I'm sorry you find that embarrassing, but I don't care anymore."

"Who's Jack?"

I looked at you. Your question had caught me off guard. How did you know about Jack? "What?"

"You heard me. Who's Jack?"

My heart was beating so loud in my chest, you could probably hear it. "How do you know about Jack?"

"Wouldn't you like to know?" you said. "Maia was scrolling through her Instagram feed, and all of a sudden she shows me this photo of you being all lovey-dovey with that guy. And then she tells me that Jack guy is another fag. Can you imagine how that felt? Having your girlfriend tell you that your best friend is spending his Friday night with a goddamn fag at a fucking gay club? And when I asked you what you were doing that night, you said you were just hanging out. How long has this been going on, Tim? How long have you been lying to me?"

"There is nothing going on!" I said, trying to keep my voice from shaking. "And we weren't being lovey-dovey."

You sneered at that, and I couldn't even blame you. Jack had taken that photo of us, of me smiling while he'd been leaning his head against my shoulder. What were you supposed to think? I didn't even bother to tell you how five minutes later, I had been stomping off in anger because Jack had behaved like an asshole. You wouldn't have believed a single word of it, and it would have only made you sneer more.

"How long, Tim? How long have you been lying to me?"

I pinched the bridge of my nose, my eyes closed as I tried fighting back the tears. "I haven't been lying to you, Tom."

"So, you're not gay? You just like hanging out with gay people? And I'm supposed to believe that?"

I shook my head. "I never said I'm not gay. I just haven't told you about it. Not telling you is not the same as lying about it."

"Oh give me a fucking break! You're gay and you didn't deem it necessary to tell your best friend? How the hell is that not lying?"

Throwing my hands in the air, I said, "Well, maybe I would have told you earlier if you weren't so …" My voice trailed off because I didn't know how to say what I wanted to say.

"If I weren't so what?"

"If you didn't hate gay people so much. I was too scared to tell you because I was afraid you'd react exactly the way you're reacting now, don't you get it?"

You scoffed. "Oh, I get it. It's my fault that you're gay now. This is fucking ridiculous!"

"That's not what I said."

"You know what, I don't care," you said, standing up and bending down to me, your face inches from mine. "Grow a pair, Tim. Grow a pair of fucking balls and then go and have them sucked on by your fucking fag friends."

You turned around and started running, not continuing on our route but back where we had come from. You didn't wait for me to run after you. You didn't turn your head to look back at me. You just ran, leaving me behind in my misery as the dam finally broke and tears started running down my face. They were tears of hurt and tears of anger. Your words had hurt me in a way I never would have thought words could hurt, and the fact those words had come from you and not some random stranger made them ever so much more scathing. I'd have taken sticks and stones every day over your brutal, merciless insults. Rocked by spastic sobs, a voice at the back of my mind whispered, 'But didn't you have it coming? Isn't this what you deserve for not coming forward earlier?' This is where my hurt mutated into defiant anger. If I ever wanted to be able to look at myself in the mirror again, I couldn't let you make me shoulder the blame for your vile verbal transgressions against me as if my fear of your reaction had been some kind of perfidious, self-serving scheme to betray your trust. Yes, I had been trying to protect myself, but I had also been trying to protect what I had always regarded as the most precious thing in my life: our friendship.

Look where it got me.

As my tears subsided and I wiped the snot from my nose with the back of my hand, I felt a daunting thought creep up on me: what if I had been wrong? What if our friendship had never been the two-way street I had made it out to be? We never had a real fight that would have put our friendship to the test, mostly because I'd always shied away from confrontation. I had always wanted it to work. I had wanted *us* to work, and whenever there had been a difference of opinion, I had rather backed down than acted up. I wasn't blaming you for that. My decisions had been mine alone, rooted in my own demure personality and nourished by my own naïveté. Pleasing you had always been more important to me than being right or having it my way. I had always wanted to have it *our* way. I hadn't realized it meant entering a deal with the devil.

I don't know how long I was sitting there, but it was a long time. I didn't want to go home and explain my swollen, reddened eyes to my parents. I didn't want to go anywhere, really, but I couldn't sit there all day wallowing in my misery. I didn't want to keep thinking about you anymore either. Deep down inside, there was a spark of hope that maybe you'd come to your senses and realize what you had done, what you had said, and that you would find it in your heart to apologize and have an honest discussion, but if that was ever going to happen, it would take days rather than hours.

When I finally got up, I felt surprisingly light, as if the burden that had been weighing down on my shoulders for way too long had been lifted. I took a couple of deep breaths to clear my head and made my way toward the exit of the park. I didn't run, I walked, my spine straight and my head held high, even if it was a reflection of how I wanted to feel rather than how I actually felt. I wanted to feel proud, and I'd be getting there, whether you or anyone else liked it or not. It was going to take some time, but I'd be getting there. Because you know what?

Something got broken when you had spat your vile insults in my face.

Something got broken.

But it hadn't been me.

Sixteen

And that's where we are. It's been five weeks, and nothing has changed. Or everything, depending on your frame of reference. If you think history started that day in the park when we last talked, then nothing has changed, and our friendship remains in a state of suspended animation. If you acknowledge, like I still do, that the history of you and I goes back our entire lives ever since we first met, then nothing is the same anymore, and it's becoming increasingly obvious to me that nothing will ever be the same again. We still see each other five out of seven days a week because we have more than half our classes together, and there's no easy way for you to completely ignore me, although I can tell you're trying your best. You say 'hi' when we pass each other in the hallway or when you take your seat at your desk next to mine in the classroom, but there's no warmth in your flat, low voice, and for the short moment you allow your eyes to meet mine, there's no twinkle, not even a fading shadow of the life we used to share. The first couple of times that you treated me like a stranger as if the only tie between us was some sort of fleeting acquaintance, I still played along, saying 'hi' back to you, timid but hopeful, trying to muster a smile that was cordial and welcoming without appearing too desperate and needy, hoping you would take the next step and accept my standing invitation to have an honest conversation.

Let's talk. Whenever you're ready.

That's the text message I sent you the day we had that talk in the park. I never got a response, and I'm no longer holding my breath. Hope springs eternal, they say, but whoever 'they' are, they're wrong. Just like I have been wrong all along.

When we were young, you always used to wrap your wiry arm around my neck and say, "Best friends forever, bro," and I believed you. I foolishly believed you, I might say today, but hindsight is 20/20. Today I know that back then, I knew nothing. *We* knew nothing. We were young and stupid, throwing around words like 'forever' without being able to grasp their meaning. Nothing springs eternal. Eternity is an awfully long time when the formerly unthinkable can become the new normal in the short span of a few weeks. For some reason you still feel compelled to say 'hi' whenever our paths cross, but where I used to return your poor excuse for a pleasantry, hoping that this time, finally, it will be the beginning of a longer conversation, I now merely acknowledge your presence with a nod or a grunt. Sometimes it feels as if even that is still more than you deserve.

I've been spending a lot of time with Inka recently. After that night we spent together in your spare bedroom, I thought I'd never be able to look her in the eyes again without wanting to crawl into a hole. But we've had a couple of pretty good talks, and it's funny how two people can bond over a shared traumatic experience. It turns out she felt just as ambushed by the stunt you and Maia pulled on us as I did. Maia told her the whole thing was a conspiracy to fix us up with each other for laughs. Not because Inka or I wanted it, but simply and solely for your own shits and giggles. But tell me again how I betrayed your trust. Because that's what you've told me, and apparently that's what you're telling people in school. I know this because I have random people asking me about it.

We both know that's not true. At least it's not the whole truth. It's funny how trust and betrayal never come up when you talk to Maia about what happened. I know this because Inka knows this. Inka knows it because she and Maia are still BFFs and talk about everything.

According to what you tell Maia, my one and only sin is being gay. Because it's unnatural and disgusting, and gays are all perverts who can't control themselves, and we're all basically out to rape innocent straight boys like you. You think it's baked into the cake because the word 'homosexuality' has the word 'sex' in it. You, on the other hand, don't see yourself as a heterosexual. No, you're 'straight' or 'normal.' You tell her how when you think about all the times I supposedly touched you, you want to take a shower because it makes you feel all icky. You tell her how sooner or later I would have come on to you, and how if that had ever happened, you would have beaten the living shit out of 'that creepy little fag.'

As if your words alone weren't painful enough, hearing them from someone else, their impact amplified tenfold by every pair of ears they went through before they reach mine, is devastating. It calls everything I ever took for granted into question, first and foremost my confidence in my own sense of judgment. My worst nightmares couldn't have painted your behavior in such chilling, horrid pictures. Should I have known better? Should I have known *you* better after all those years? It's not as if the signals weren't there. I knew how you feel about gay people. Why do you think I was so reluctant to tell you? Nevertheless, I thought maybe your opinion on gay people was rooted in ignorance. I thought that maybe you'd think different about gay people once you realized you've known a gay guy for twelve years. Maybe it was naïve of me to think our friendship carried enough clout to sway your opinion. I never would have thought your hatred could outweigh everything I thought we had, but here we are. For so many years I've been forgiving of you and your antics in a way I would have liked you to be forgiving when it really mattered. Maybe I was expecting too much.

It's becoming ever more evident to me that I never stood a reasonable chance to emerge unscathed from this drama that is in part farce, in part tragedy. I chose to do the right thing, only to see everything we had and everything we could never have disappear in the coldest depths of an indifferent universe. But what was the alternative? Had I not come out to you, my secret would have been a stain on our friendship forever, invisible to you yet glaringly obvious to me. I could have saved our friendship, the deepest friendship I have ever known, by living a perpetual lie, by pretending to be a different person than I am, by striving to be the person you wanted me to be. It might have worked for you, but I never would have been able to look you in the eyes again the way I always used to.

Those damn beautiful, twinkling eyes, deep and blue like the ocean. There were days when I was nearly drowning in your eyes but then you'd catch my rapturous gaze and frown at me and say, "What are you looking at, you creep?" Then I would shake my head and laugh it off, pretending your words didn't hurt. But hurt they did, and sometimes you would notice. Then you would say, "Come here, you creep," and wrap your arm around my neck and ruffle my hair until I smiled again, only to exploit my weakness and turn your hair-ruffling into a noogie. Ever so often, play begot pain, and I would play along, addicted to your every bit of attention, good or bad, perhaps mistaking your lighthearted abuse for affection, perhaps mistaking your abuse as lighthearted. Physically, I never stood a chance against your brawn, my Jell-o muscles no match for yours made of steel. But I knew your Achilles' heel. Trapped in your headlock, your pointy knuckles mauling my scalp, I would put my hands on your sides and claw my fingers into your waist. My delicate fingers were always stronger than your clenched fists as they rendered you helplessly gasping for air, your tears of uncontrollable laughter blinding those dazzling blue eyes as I submitted you to that special kind of torture. It was the one and only power I wielded over you, that sweet, delicious, inebriating power, always tempting me to overplay my hand. One step too far and your laughter would turn into a scowl, a scary, menacing glare. Unleashing that carefully concealed potential for violence, you would lash out like a wounded animal ready to kill if that's what it took to survive. It only happened once or twice, but your outbursts never failed to leave a lasting impression. "I hit a door frame," I used to explain the bruises on my arm away to my parents, silently accepting the bruises on my soul. *I probably deserved it*, I would tell myself, accepting my compunction as a necessary result of my loss of self-control, the inevitable hangover after getting drunk with power.

You never got hangovers from your binging on power. Over the years you built up a tolerance, like an alcoholic, and your intoxication became your natural state, your dominance forever unchallenged. I used to be fine with that. You were a natural born leader, and ever so often your boisterous rambunctiousness served both as my armor and my weapon. With you by my side I felt bold and invincible, ready to take on challenges I never would have dared to seek on my own, basking in a glory that was all yours. Some people didn't even know my name. To them I was just 'Tom's friend'. I was fine with that. It even filled me with conceited, narcissistic pride because I had what others were secretly longing for. You were my friend, my ally, my confidant. You could have picked anyone to be your best friend. There never was a shortage of eager candidates. But you chose me. I never understood why, but I always shied away from pursuing the question lest I find myself confronted with an inconvenient truth I didn't want to know. Whatever it was we had, I didn't want it to end, because it felt so good, so comforting, so empowering. I was standing on the shoulders of a giant, and I loved it because I loved you.

You're cringing at my use of the L-word now. I know you are. Even when Maia clings to your arm and her lips seek the soft touch of your neck, you shy away, your ears on fire, your awkward cringe eventually morphing into an irritated frown, and I always hope she finds the right moment to let go of you before she pushes you over the brink and you lash out at her. I used to find your clumsy handling of all sorts of public displays of affection cute, appealing even, as you aspired to that reactionary epitome of masculinity. Be tough, be strong, show no emotion, no sign of weakness. Always act like you're in control of the situation even if you have no freaking clue what's going on. Always strive to be in control of others just like you pretend to be in control of yourself.

At twelve, you would say "Best friends forever, bro," and put your arm around my neck, and I would lean my head against yours, knowing full well that my display of affection would end me up in a headlock, your knuckles scouring my scalp. It was a price I was ready to pay for feeling close to you.

At fourteen, you would say "Best friends forever, bro," and punch my arm, a little too hard to be unequivocally affectionate, a little too rowdy to be cute. Nevertheless, I would lean into you, to seek comfort and to give you the chance to dispel my doubts, but you would shrink back, the sparkle in your eyes murked by the dark shadow of a suspicious frown.

Over the years something has changed, and I never understood what it was. Was it just testosterone, or was it social conventions and expectations that compelled you to protect your fragile ego by aspiring to some archaic stereotype of masculinity? Was it something new, or did puberty just amplify what had always been there? Maybe you've always been you, just like I like to think I've always been me, and now we're just both even more so. Have we, for all those years, only ever seen in each other what we wanted to see, and now that our eyes have been opened to a broader, more refined truth, we've become disillusioned and disappointed? I'm not sure I will ever find out the answer to this question. I'm not sure if I even want to. Before long, my memories will be all I have left of my time with you, and if they let me, if *you* let me, I would rather love than loathe them. Just like I would still, even after everything that happened, rather love than loathe you. Even if you maybe don't deserve it. Even if you're not making it easy.

The last couple of weeks have been pretty strange, and not just because of you. Sadly, you don't have a monopoly on homophobia and bigotry. I never made any kind of official announcement about my sexuality, and I'm not going to, because quite frankly it's none of anyone's business. But I'm no longer actively keeping it a secret, and that's all it took to spread the word. At school, I'm mostly hanging out with Aidan and his friends now. Aidan doesn't conceal his affection for me in public, nor do I shy away from it, so everyone with half a brain can figure out what that means. Some people ask me, "Are you gay?" just to be sure, and when they do I say yes. Most people are cool with that, and I'm cool with that, too. Some have come up to me to tell me my demeanor has changed. They say I'm more outgoing now, and they see me laugh or smile more often. Maybe it's because I no longer have to ponder every single word before I say it, and I no longer have to restrain every gesture, every expression when I'm excited about something because it might make me look too fabulous. I no longer have to hide who I really am, and it's a liberating feeling.

But it's not all rainbows and unicorns here in gayland. Not everyone likes gay people, and that's fine because no one likes everyone, and I don't like everyone either. I still believe we could all get along if we really wanted to, though. Sadly, not everyone wants to. The other day, I walked into Mrs. Garcia's geography class to find a banana with a condom over it on my desk. You know this because you were sitting at the desk right next to mine. Some people thought that was a really hilarious prank, and even you didn't bother to conceal the stupid grin on your face. I didn't think it was all that funny, to be honest. What bothered me the most about it, though, was how it yet again made me question my judgment. I'm not accusing you of having put that banana on my desk. For old times' sake I'm willing to give you the benefit of the doubt, and despite everything that happened, I still don't think you'd go that low. But you didn't do anything about it either. You just sat there and let me walk into the room to be humiliated and laughed at. After our talk in the park, this was the toughest and most devastating moment for me because that was when it became painfully clear to me that everything we had means nothing to you. I'm no longer sure it ever did.

The reason I'm telling you all these things I'd once sworn you'd never find out is because I can hardly make things worse. You already have the worst possible impression of my true intentions, so I might as well be honest. In hindsight, and it is all hindsight now, all of my unrequited love's labor is lost. All my painful efforts to curb my burning feelings of love and desire for the sake of our friendship were in vain. "'Tis better to have loved and lost than never to have loved at all,' Tennyson says, and I know you will sneer at me for quoting poetry to you, but you will be missing the point. The point is, and perhaps I'm trying to convince myself here rather than you, is that I have loved and lost. Whether it is better than never to have loved you at all, I don't know. What I do know, though, is that I'm still struggling to come to terms with the feeling of having nothing left to lose for I've already lost you.

Seventeen

"Happy Birthday, sweetheart, and many happy returns," Milo says, placing a pink cupcake with rainbow colored frosting and a single burning candle in front of me. "This one's on the house."

I pull the cupcake toward me. "Thanks, Milo. That's so sweet of you."

"You're very welcome," he says, distributing our milkshakes.

Aidan puts his hand on my leg and squeezes it gently, leaning into me. I turn my head and let him kiss me on the lips. "Happy Birthday, babe."

"Thanks," I say with a sigh. "Again." I look across the table at Inka and Chris. "I swear, this is, like, the twentieth time he's wished me a happy birthday today. I feel like I should be thirty-seven by now."

Milo issues a short, sardonic laugh. "Oh please," he says, looking at me. "Let me say this as a balding, middle aged man: I am personally offended by your pristine, unadulterated youth. That goes for all of you, by the way. Having said that, I don't begrudge it to you. So enjoy it while it lasts, because it won't last forever, even if it may feel that way sometimes."

"Poor Milo," Chris says. "You don't look a day over thirty, if that makes you feel better."

Milo shakes his head. "It doesn't, because it's a lie. Nice try, though." Clutching his empty tray under his arm, he turns on his heel and makes his way back behind the counter.

With both my hands on the table and a stupid, giddy grin on my face, I look at the twisted pink and white candle with its small flickering flame before I take a deep breath and blow it out. As Inka and Chris cheer and applaud, Aidan smiles at me and says, "Did you make a wish?"

I nod. "I asked for—"

I don't get to finish my sentence, because everyone freaks out and Aidan hurries to place one hand in my neck and the other across my mouth.

"No!"

"Dude!"

"Whoa!"

Looking back and forth between their aghast faces, I slowly raise my hands in defeat until Aidan finally removes his hand from my mouth.

"What did I—"

"You're not supposed to say it!"

"You'll jinx it!"

"What is wrong with you?"

"Wow, okay," I say, "I didn't know you guys were so superstitious."

Inka's jaw drops, Chris puts his hand on his forehead, and Aidan playfully slaps my arm.

"If you're not superstitious, why did you even make a wish?"

"Because I'm only a little superstitious?" I say with a shrug.

Aidan scoffs. "That doesn't even make any sense."

"Sure it does," I say, pulling the candle from the cupcake and dropping it on the table. "Besides, peer pressure. Everyone does it, and if I hadn't done it, I never would have heard the end of it from *you*."

Looking across the table, he says, "See what I have to put up with every day?"

"Thoughts and prayers," Chris says. "Where the heck did you even find this guy?"

Aidan glares at Chris. "*Someone* dragged him into the Unicorn Club one day."

Turning his head to glare at Inka, Chris says, "*Someone* told me the kid needed help."

"Don't pin this on me, guys," Inka says with a dismissive wave of her hand. "I did the right thing. When you find a stray puppy and you can't keep it, you hand it over to a shelter and hope it'll find a responsible, loving family. So there."

We all glare at her.

I raise an eyebrow. "I'm a stray puppy now?"

"More like a gay puppy," Aidan says, and I cast him a grimacing smile.

"Sam and I have talked about adoption," Chris says. "But this is not how we imagined it."

Inka throws her hands in the air. "Guys! I was speaking metaphorically. The loving family I was talking about is the gay community. Come on now, it's not rocket science."

"Oh, good," Chris says, looking at me. "For a moment I thought we'd have to give you food and shelter and mop your pee off the kitchen floor."

Aidan and Inka burst out laughing.

Patting my head, Aidan says, "Who's a good boy?"

Swatting his hand away, I say, "I keep hearing how great it is to have a bunch of really good friends. I should probably try it sometime."

My quip earns me fake hisses and jeers, followed by genuine giggles and smiles as I take a bite of my birthday cupcake. Aidan wraps his wiry arm around my neck, pulls me close and ruffles my hair. It's funny how you can have rituals with different people that are so similar, yet so different. The first couple of times he put his arm around me and ruffled my hair, I would almost freak out. It was just too eerie. But he would leave it at that. Just ruffle my hair, kiss me on the head, and let go of me again. No noogies, no taunts, no bruising punches to my arm. It took me a while to get used to it, and even now, I still twitch sometimes, getting ready to claw my fingers in his side to fend him off, but I never have to.

"Get a room, you two," Chris says with a grin.

"No!" Inka nudges him with her elbow. "I want to see this."

He looks at her, but before he gets to say anything, I gasp because I just remembered something.

"Oh my God, you guys," I say, putting the half-eaten cupcake back on the table, "you have no idea what happened last weekend." I turn to Aidan. "I haven't even told you this yet."

"Uh-oh, this can't be good."

"Yeah, no, nothing bad, just super awkward." I turn back to Inka and Chris. "So, my parents went out on a date last Saturday night, and Aidan was over at my place and … um, fast forward, some time after ten he was about to leave because we figured my parents would be back soon, and indeed, the moment he walked out the front door, my parents were getting out of their car. They exchanged a few pleasantries with Aidan and said good night."

"Perfect timing," Aidan says.

174

I shake my head. "Wait for it. Anyway, they came inside, but they were behaving kinda weird. I thought maybe the date didn't go as planned or they had been fighting or something. But the next morning everything seemed to be fine again, so I didn't think much of it. Okay, so today I asked my mom if it's okay for Aidan to sleep over tonight, and her reaction was super weird. She was hemming and hawing and beating around the bush, so I asked her what's wrong."

Aidan winces. "I don't like where this is going."

"No, you don't," I say, looking at him. "Last weekend, when you were leaving and they got out of the car ... well, they'd been sitting there for forty minutes."

Inka is the first to get it. "Oh my God."

"What?" Aidan says with a confused frown on his face. "Why?"

"Because they came home, and when they entered the house they heard us. From my bedroom. As we were ... you know, doing things."

As Inka and Chris crack up, slapping their thighs, Aidan's face turns a dark crimson. "Oh. My. God."

I nod. "I know, right? They didn't know what to do, so they got back in the car and waited for you to leave."

"It's kind of sweet, really," Inka says.

Aidan looks at me. "Well, I guess you know what that means." When I shrug and shake my head, he adds, "It means I can never look your parents in the eyes again, or even be in the same room with them or I will die of embarrassment!"

I chuckle and stroke his glowing cheek with the back of my hand. "Don't be silly now, babe. It's fine. My parents were more embarrassed than you are. But we talked about it, and everything's fine. You can sleep over tonight."

"Yay," he says, devoid of any enthusiasm.

"We should probably keep the noise down, though."

He winces again, making us all laugh.

"Parents these days," Chris says, shaking his head.

As I finish my cupcake and we continue to banter and drink our milkshakes, I repeatedly check my phone. I know that the message I'm waiting for but at the same time expecting not to come isn't there, because I would have noticed the push notification, but I feel the need to be sure. Inka casts me a furtive glance every time I peek at my phone. She knows what's happening—or not happening—but she's kind enough not to rub salt into what is still an open wound, and I'm not going to bring it up because the likely take that 'he probably just forgot' is not something I want to hear. You didn't forget my birthday. Your birthday is exactly a week before mine. I even sent you a text message.

Happy Birthday, Tom. I'm still here if you want to talk.

After composing the message, I spent about half an hour mulling whether to send it or delete it. I didn't want to seem desperate and defile my newly found pride, but knowing how stubborn you can be, I wanted to make one last-ditch effort to reach out to you. I don't know what, if anything, I was expecting, but your reply made it painfully clear that whatever little it may have been, it was too much.

Thanks.

That was it. You couldn't have made it any clearer that you no longer have any interest in me or us or talking things through. So why do I keep checking my phone? I don't know. I guess part of me still thinks so highly of you that I think you might return the courtesy and wish me a happy birthday too, but I won't be surprised if I'm in for yet another disappointment. It would be the last one, though, of that I'm sure.

"So what did he get you?" Inka says in my direction.

"Hm?" I say, not immediately aware what she's referring to.

"Your boyfriend. He did get you something for your birthday, I hope?"

"Oh!" I say, "Yes! *Dear Evan Hansen* tickets. It's playing in L.A. in November. I'm super excited."

"Nice," Inka says.

Chris nods in agreement. "I'm jealous."

"You better be nice to me then," I say. "I got two tickets, and I haven't decided who I'm gonna take with me yet."

Aidan's loud gasp makes me turn my head to look at him. "Did you say something, honey?"

"How *dare* you?" he says in a low voice, an expression of mock shock on his face.

"What?" I say, struggling to keep a straight face because across the table, Inka and Chris are already cracking up.

Aidan looks at me with sad puppy eyes, his bottom lip starting to quiver. It's an adorable sight to behold, but it's also too heartbreaking to bear for an extended period of time, so I let my deadpan face break into a smile, wrap my arm around his shoulders and pull him toward me for a tight squeeze. The way we treat each other, tease each other, cherish each other is so different from anything that ever happened between you and me. You'd never have allowed the kind of role play where for just a few moments I'd get to be the one in control, because you can't stand even the slightest appearance of weakness or humility, even if it's just pretend. One should never compare a current relationship to one's exes, or so I've heard, because apparently it's not fair to anyone. I guess it's a good thing we never were lovers then, and I get to compare anyone I like to the biggest love that never was. Call me petty if you like, but maybe I need this to convince myself that I'm better off without you. I'm not a flawless human being, and I'm not expecting anyone else to be, but the relief of no longer being around someone who thinks he is has finally outgrown the sense of loss.

After kissing Aidan on the cheek, I take another peek at my phone, and when I place it back on the table, my gaze floats across the street toward the entrance of the mall where you're having an animated conversation with Maia. Seeing you makes my heart jump, and not in a good way. It's not a jump for joy. It's more like the kind of jump people make when they discover a giant spider on their bathroom ceiling or when a rat scurries across their patio. There's a lump in my throat I want to swallow but can't because my mouth is all dried up, so I take a couple of deep breaths through my nose instead.

As always, Inka is the first to notice something's not right. "You okay, Tim?"

"I don't know," I say, my eyes still trained on you and Maia.

Inka follows my gaze across the street where she sees Maia gesturing with her arms as she's talking to you. You listen, looking miffed, your hands deep in your pockets.

"Uh-oh," Inka says, and Aidan and Chris finally catch on, leaning across the table to see what the fuss is all about.

"Oh," Chris says, "is that—"

"Yes," Aidan cuts him off, and from the tone in his voice I can tell he's upset. I'm not sure if he's upset on my behalf or on his own.

I put my hand on his and squeeze it. "It's okay. Don't worry about it."

"Are you sure?"

I nod, still peering across the street.

"They're not gonna come over, are they?" Aidan says, and he sounds as anxious as I feel, and about the same thing, too.

"I don't know."

Inka says, "I think Maia wants to but Tom doesn't," and as if on cue, Maia grabs your hand and starts dragging you toward the traffic light at the intersection.

Aidan is squeezing my hand now, and when I turn my head, he casts me a pitiful look as if he wants to tell me that in some kind of freak accident, my pet goldfish somehow got flushed down the toilet.

"Relax," I say. "I'm not gonna make a scene."

He nods. "What about him, though?"

"Um," Chris says as you and Maia make your way across the street, "should we, like, give you some privacy or something?"

Inka snorts. "I'm not going anywhere. He may need witnesses."

"Guys, relax, okay? It's gonna be fine," I say, but I'm really just trying to convince myself.

As you and Maia walk past our window, she waves at me with an excited grin on her face while you keep your eyes straight ahead as if you haven't even noticed we're here. Sometimes I'm envious of your ability to be cold and detached. Then again, it's a character trait that would make me a completely different person.

As you and Maia enter the Korova, she lets go of your hand and comes running toward me. Aidan jumps up from his seat and squeezes next to Chris and Inka on the opposite side of the table. I move to Aidan's vacated seat, but I don't have time to get up before Maia throws herself around my neck.

"Happy Birthday, Tim," she says, planting a kiss on my cheek and rubbing my back.

I pat her back. "Thanks, Maia."

She lets go of me, turns to the others and waves her hand. "Hi, guys." As you slowly approach me, your hands in your pockets, Maia looks at Aidan and reaches out her hand. "You must be Tim's boyfriend. I'm Maia."

"Yes," Aidan says, casting a glance at me as if he wants to make sure he's allowed to exchange pleasantries with the girl-friend of my ex best friend. I flash him a brief smile, and he shakes her hand. "Aidan."

I turn my head, and there you are, standing right in front of me and trying your hardest not to make eye contact with anyone. You clear your throat and say, "Hi," to no one in particular.

"Hi," I say in the most neutral voice I can muster but glar-ing you straight in the eyes as if I'm looking for something. Or anything, really.

You pull your hand out of your pocket and stretch it out toward me, your movements sluggish and heavy as if some-thing is weighing you down. "Happy Birthday," you say as I shake your hand that's cold and flaccid like a dead fish.

"Thanks," I say in a low voice. Our eyes briefly meet, but you quickly break away. After a few excruciating seconds of awkward silence, I say, "Wanna sit?"

You shake your head. "No, uh … we were on our way to the mall and we saw you guys sitting here, so we thought we'd pop over real quick so say hi and, you know, Happy Birthday."

"Right," I say. "Well, thanks again."

"All right."

"So, what are you guys up to?" Maia asks.

"Nothing much," I say. "Finish up here and then we're off clubbing."

"Oh, okay."

"It's *Sparkles* night at the Unicorn Club," Inka helpfully adds, and by casting an empty glance out of the window you make a point of pretending not to know what that is or what it means.

I look at Inka, and her smile is not all that subtle. She totally brought up the Unicorn Club in an attempt to troll you, and I suddenly feel emboldened, so I turn to Maia and say, "You should come."

From the corner of my eye I can see you wince, anxious for Maia to give the right answer.

"Yeah," Maia says. "But … you know."

"Yeah," I say, smiling. "I know."

You've finally reached a level of discomfort you can no longer bear, so you turn to Maia. "Shall we?"

Maia nods. She gives my another hug, rubbing my back. "You guys have fun, okay?"

"Definitely," I say. As I pat her back, your gaze briefly meets mine again, and finally, for the first time since you walked in here, a shadow of authenticity flashes across your face as you can no longer conceal the contempt in your eyes, dispelling the last doubts I may have had until just now. You're sticking to your guns, and that's fine because I know you can't help yourself. I am finally sticking to my own guns, too. To quote you quoting Robert E. Lee: never do a wrong thing to make a friend or to keep one. I cannot change who I am. I'm no longer expecting you to change who you are. At least now I know for sure where we're at, and I can finally move on. Maybe you can, too.

Maia breaks away from me, waves to the table, and as soon as she takes your hand, you turn on your heel and pull her away.

"Bye, guys," Milo sounds from behind the counter, polishing a glass.

"Bye," Maia says, and once you're out of the door, we all breathe a collective sigh of relief.

"Dude!" Chris says. "No offense, but I hate that guy."

I shake my head and continue eating my cupcake. "None taken."

"I wanted to punch his pretty face," Aidan says, and I pat his thigh.

Chris snorts. "I wanted to kick him in the nuts."

Aidan looks at me. "Are you okay?"

Looking back at him, I nod. "I'm fine. Don't worry."

With his finger, he wipes a crumb from the corner of my mouth and licks it off. "Mmh, chocolate."

"Thanks, Mom," I say, rolling my eyes, and he leans into me for a quick kiss.

Chris finishes his milkshake and looks at his watch. "All right, you guys, I better get going. Gotta pick up Sam from work and then pull Jack out of the gutter. We'll meet you at the Unicorn, okay?"

"All right," I say.

He looks at Inka. "Are you coming with us or …?"

She nods and empties her glass.

Chris peers out the window across the street where you and Maia are about to enter the mall. "If we hurry, maybe we get to run him over."

I shake my head and chuckle. "Yeah, don't do that."

He sighs.

"See you guys at the club," Inka says, and they both leave.

Aidan and I continue sitting there for a while longer, sipping our milkshakes, his head on my shoulder, my hand on his. We don't talk. There's not much to say, and we don't have to talk to enjoy each other's company.

In the car on our way to the Unicorn, Aidan keeps casting furtive glances at me from the corner of his eye until I finally say, "Aidan?"

"What?"

"Stop looking at me like that. I'm okay, okay?"

With a sheepish grin, he says, "All right, all right. Just making sure."

"Right."

"How did you know what I was thinking?"

"I can read your mind," I say. "Didn't you know?"

"Is that right?" He stops at a red light and looks at me. "What am I thinking now?"

I look him deep in the eyes for a few moments, then I gasp and say, "You pervert!"

"Wow, you're good," he says, his face flushing, and we laugh all the way to the club.

When we pull into the parking lot, Chris and Sam's car is already there, so we make our way inside, walking into a thick wall of hot and humid air that's vibrating with hard beats and radiating with multicolored strobe lights. It's only my third time here, but the place already feels as familiar as my own bedroom. As comfortable, too, because unlike any other place outside my bedroom and maybe the Korova, I can be myself and I don't feel like I have to pretend to be anything or anyone I'm not. I can act the way it feels natural for me to act, and no one will give a damn or look at me funny. Around here, nobody cares if you have blue hair, as some people do, or piercings in unorthodox places. Around here, I'm not scared of anyone, because I know no one will judge me or bully me or ridicule me for who I am. And around here, everyone else feels exactly the same. This is our island. This is where we want to be because it's where we can be.

The place is crowded as ever. There is no point in wandering around trying to find the others. The easiest way to find them is to stay in one place and wait for them to find us, so Aidan takes me by the hand and leads me onto the dance floor. We laugh, we sing, we dance, our eyes open, our eyes closed. Maybe twenty minutes, maybe thirty, maybe an hour. Who can tell, and who cares? Time stands still when yesterday no longer matters and tomorrow is still but a distant dream. Happiness is when it's only the here and now that counts. At one point, Aidan's face lights up as he gazes past me, and before I have time to turn around, someone wraps their arms around me from behind and squeezes me, pressing their cheek against mine.

"Happy Birthday!" Sam shouts over the music into my ear. He briefly releases me so I can turn around, then he flings his arms around my neck for another tight hug. Behind him, Chris and Inka smile at me.

"Thank you!"

"You're almost a big boy now," Sam says. "You still don't look a day over twelve, though."

With a grin on my lips, I roll my eyes. "That joke never gets old, does it?"

"Just like you," Sam says, and we both laugh.

He lets go of me, and both Chris and Inka hug me again as if they haven't seen me in weeks. We dance, we sing, we laugh. Maybe fifteen minutes, maybe twenty. Nobody can tell, and nobody cares. After a while, nature calls, so I tell Aidan and make my way to the restrooms. On my way back, I stop at the bar. Before I get to order, I hear a voice next to me.

"Hey there, stranger."

I cast a quick glance to the side, just long enough to see it's Jack. We haven't met or talked since our little altercation here at the club a couple of weeks back, and somewhere deep inside, I'm still holding a grudge. It's not small enough to forget, but not big enough to wear on my sleeve, so I raise an eyebrow at him and say, "Are you hitting on me?"

He scoffs. "Dude, you're a minor. Do I look like I want to go to jail?"

"Just checking," I say.

"I hear it's your birthday today, is that right?"

I nod. "So my parents tell me."

"Well, Happy Birthday."

"Thanks."

"Let me buy you a drink."

I shake my head. "Thanks, but I'm good."

"I insist."

"You really don't have to," I say, finally looking at him to emphasize my point. That's when I see his black eye. "Yikes, what happened to your face?"

He winces. "I got beat up, okay? And I know I don't have to buy you a drink, but it's your birthday and I want to. I'm making a fucking effort here, so why can't you just say 'Sure, thanks, Jack,' and roll with it?"

I look at him. The subtle anger in his voice doesn't match the sadness in his eyes. "All right," I finally say.

He smiles. "There you go. Now that wasn't so hard, was it?"

He orders us two energy drinks and hands one to me.

"Thanks, Jack."

"Don't mention it."

I take a couple of swigs from my can.

"Wanna step outside for a minute?" Jack says.

I'd rather go back to Aidan and the others, but I feel for Jack. He seems thin-skinned and vulnerable, much more than last time, and he's obviously still making an effort to be nice, for whatever reason, so I shrug and say, "Sure."

I follow his lead to the outdoor terrace. Once again, we sit on the bench next to the large butt bin, and Jack offers me a cigarette.

I shake my head. "Still not smoking."

"Good for you," he says, lighting one up. "Smoking kills, you know?"

"I know. So why do you smoke then?"

He looks at me with a nonchalant smile. "Because smoking kills?"

"Surely there must be quicker ways to kill yourself."

He takes a long drag, exhaling smoke as he says, "Who says I want to die quickly? I'm young, I want to live my life. Just not too long."

"So, you're going for a slow and painful death?"

"Life is gonna be painful no matter what you do. It'll always find a way to kick you in the nuts or punch you in the face or whatever."

I stare at his black eye until he finally says, "What?"

"Wanna tell me what happened to your eye?"

"It was your fault, really," he says with a smirk. "Kind of."

"What?" I frown. "What did *I* do?"

"You called me a hypocrite for the way I handled being gay. Said I had no self-respect."

"Well, not that I want to relitigate that whole thing, but I was right, wasn't I?"

He looks me straight in the eyes. "Yes."

"I'm glad you realized that. So you got mad at yourself and punched yourself in the face or something?"

He flashes me a wry smile and says, "I came out to my parents. My dad didn't take it well." He sticks the cigarette in his mouth and lifts his T-shirt to show me his torso. His left side is littered with violet bruises, some of them already turned yellow.

I gasp. "Jesus Christ!"

He looks down at himself, ashes from his cigarette falling on his pants. "I know, right?"

"I'm sorry," I say in a low voice.

"Don't worry about it." He drops his T-shirt, brushes the ashes from his pants and takes another drag of his cigarette. "I was kidding when I said it was your fault. I'm not blaming you or anything. It was bound to happen sooner or later anyway."

After a pause I say, "How can he do something like that?"

Jack snorts. "My dad doesn't need a reason to beat me up. He's been doing it my entire life. And being the obnoxious little fuck that I am, I probably deserve it, too."

"Don't say that," I say.

He shrugs, picking at a scab on the back of his hand. "It's okay. I'm gonna be okay."

"You better," I say, nudging him with my elbow.

"Yeah, don't worry." He takes one final drag before he tosses his cigarette into the giant butt bin. Exhaling smoke through his nostrils, he leans back against the wall behind us and stares up at the starry night sky.

"I'm proud of you, you know?" I say.

"Don't patronize me," Jack says, his apathetic tone suggesting he doesn't really mind me patronizing him.

"I am, though. I mean, surely you must have known your dad wasn't going to take it well."

"Of course. Why do you think it took me that long?"

"And yet you went ahead and did it anyway. It takes guts. I kinda know what I'm talking about."

He exhales. "Yeah, well."

"Your dad may not respect you, but at least you do."

"All right, all right, stop already," he says. "If I need a blow job, I'll let you know."

I shrug. "I'm just saying."

"All right." He looks at me. "Chris told me about you and Troy."

"Ted," I say.

Not getting the joke, Jack looks puzzled. "What?"

"Never mind," I say with a chuckle. "Tom. His name is Tom."

"Right, Tom. So, you're done with him now?"

"More like he's done with me, but yeah. Same difference."

"Good for you."

"Yeah, well. I'm lucky I got other friends. Without them, I'd probably feel pretty devastated right now."

"Really? You got friends?" he deadpans, but it doesn't take long for him to crack up. I playfully slap his arm. He puts his hand on my neck and strokes my nape with his thumb. "I like you."

"Thanks. I like you too," I say, and I think I actually mean it.

He looks at me with a serene smile for a few moments. Then, without a warning, he wraps his arm around my neck, pulls me into a headlock and gives me a gentle noogie. I waste no time and dig my fingers into his waist, making him jump and squeal. We play fight for a few moments until I manage to break free, and we end up laughing at each other like a bunch of ten-year-olds.

"Are we interrupting anything?"

I turn my head to see Aidan standing in front of us, his eyebrows raised, but a smile on his face. Behind him, Inka, Chris and Sam are eying us curiously.

Jack shakes his head. "Nope. Just putting the little twerp in his place. Come sit." He stands, offering Aidan his seat. I get up too, but I rise too quickly and suddenly feel dizzy.

"Whoa," Aidan says, holding me as I sway. "You drunk or something?"

Blinking, I shake my head. "I think I danced too much. Should have eaten more than just a cupcake."

"Come sit."

He sits on the bench, but instead of sitting next to him, I turn and lie down, putting my feet on the bench and my head in Aidan's lap. "Sorry, guys, I need to lie down for a minute."

"That's all right," Chris says, sitting down on the ground. The others join him, sitting in a semi-circle around the bench.

Cradling my head in his lap, Aidan looks down at me. "Poor baby. Shall we get you some pizza later?"

"Oh yes, please."

"All right then." He looks at the others. "Anyone else feeling famished?"

"Yeah."

"Oh, yes."

"Fuck yeah."

"Me too."

"Great," Aidan says. "It's Tim's birthday. He's buying."

There are cheers all around.

"Uh," I say, raising my head, but Aidan puts his hand on my chest to keep me down.

"Shhh," he says. "You don't have to say anything. We know how much like us."

Looking him in the eyes, I say, "I don't think you do."

"No?"

I shake my head. "No."

He kisses my forehead, then my lips.

"Get a room, you two," Sam says.

"Yeah," Jack says, "or a bathroom stall!"

Inka groans. "Jack!"

"What? Bathroom stalls are way underrated. Trust me."

Inka shudders. "I'm dying for a shower stall right now," she says, making us all chuckle.

I no longer feel dizzy, but I don't want to sit up. I'm feeling too comfortable just lying there, snuggled up against Adan's groin, his hand on my stomach, the other stroking my hair as playful banter keeps going back and forth. I'm among friends, and while it may say more about myself and my previous life than about them, I can't help but think they're the best friends I've ever had.

As Aidan leans back against the wall, his hand still on my stomach, I get a clear view of the night sky. Listening to my friends' chatter and the distant beat of the music, I start counting stars when out of nowhere, a shooting star appears.

"Shooting star!" I say, and everyone looks up.

It's a big one, alight long enough for everyone to catch a glimpse before it fades.

"So pretty," Sam says.

Aidan holds me a little tighter.

"Did you guys make a wish?" Inka says.

"Yeah," Chris says, leaning his head against Sam's shoulder.

"Me too," Sam says.

Smiling at me, Aidan says, "Me too."

"Guys," I say, "do shooting stars grant multiple wishes? I mean, a wish for everyone who sees it, or only one wish for the person who spots it first? Asking for a friend."

"Dude," Chris says, "you already got your wish when you blew out the candle on your cupcake."

I turn my head to wink at him. "But the shooting star doesn't know that."

"Shooting stars know everything," Aidan says.

"I think shooting stars grant wishes to everyone who sees them," Inka says.

Sam nods, still staring at the sky. "Yeah."

Jack scoffs. "I think shooting stars are rocks from outer space that burn to death when they enter the earth's atmosphere."

We all glare at him as Inka slaps his arm. "Jack!"

"Dude," Chris says, "way to kill the mood."

"What?" Jack says. "It's basic science, bitches! You guys still believe in Santa, too?"

We exchange shocked looks before we turn to him and say in unison, "Yes!"

Jack shakes his head. "Whatever. You're all crazy, and I'm the only grown up here."

"If that's what it means to be a grown up," Sam says, "I hope I'll never grow up."

Chris kisses his cheek. "You can grow up and still believe in Santa."

Sam looks at him. "And fairies?"

"And fairies."

"And unicorns," Inka says.

"Fuck yeah, unicorns!" I say.

Aidan looks down at me with a smile. "Do you believe in unicorns?"

"I *am* a unicorn."

"Oh yeah?" He grazes my forehead with his fingertips.

I frown at him. "What are you doing?"

"Looking for your horn."

"Yeah, wrong place," I say, and I'm not even embarrassed to say something so sleazy.

Aidan laughs and kisses me on the forehead. "You're adorable."

"Oh yeah?"

"Yeah."

We kiss. It's a long kiss, and when we break away, I look at the others. Sam and Chris are kissing. Jack and Inka are both

191

lying on the ground, their heads next to each other, chatting quietly. As Aidan leans back against the wall, closing his eyes and gently stroking my hair, I turn my head toward the sky again to look for another shooting star.

I still got so many wishes.

Thank you for reading *Never do a Wrong Thing.* If you enjoyed it, a quick review over at Amazon and/or Goodreads would be greatly appreciated. Reviews help authors make a living and write more books.

Younger versions of Chris and Jack appeared in the novel *Cupid Painted Blind.* You may want to check it out if you haven't already done so.

About the Author

Marcus Herzig, future bestselling author and professional cynic, was born in 1970 and studied Law, English, Educational Science, and Physics, albeit none of them with any tenacity or ambition. After dropping out of university he held various positions in banking, utilities, and Big Oil that bore no responsibility or decision-making power whatsoever.

Always destined to be a demiurge, Marcus has been inventing characters and telling stories since the age of five. His favorite genre, both as a reader and a writer, is Young Adult literature, but he also very much enjoys science- and literary fiction.

Marcus, who finds it very peculiar to talk about himself in the third person, prefers sunsets over sunrises, white wine over red, beer over wine, pizza over pasta, and humanity over humans. His favorite person is his future husband. Their favorite place is the beach.

Also by Marcus Herzig

Instafamous
Counterparts
Cupid Painted Blind
Eschaton - The Beginning
Idolism

www.marcus-herzig.com
Follow the author on Twitter @Marcus_Herzig

MARCUS HERZIG

Cupid
Painted
Blind

Few things are more exciting and, frankly, unnerving than your first day of high school. Except, maybe, coming out to your friends when they already kinda knew you were gay. Or finding out that the breathtakingly handsome guy you've just met is best buddies with your archnemesis who happens to be a homophobic bully. Or being teamed up for a school assignment with that decidedly unattractive, facially-deformed, freaky-looking weirdo who hasn't got a friend in the world. Or all of the above.

Matthew Dunstan, closeted freshman, future bestselling author, and frequently blushing teenager is on a quest to find himself, find love, and live happily ever after. Sounds easy enough, right? But when the opportunities for failure are endless, it doesn't take much to turn your life upside down. And that's not exactly what you need when you try to catch someone's eye without attracting everyone's attention.

Cupid Painted Blind is a heartbreaking, heartwarming, and occasionally hilarious roller coaster ride through an awkward freshman's first few weeks of high school that will appeal to readers of all ages who enjoy Young Adult LGBTQ fiction.

ISBN: 978-1537704869

35275942R00118

Made in the USA
Middletown, DE
04 February 2019